THE DARK LORD
OF PENGERSICK

THE DARK LORD OF PENGERSICK

by

Richard Carlyon

FARRAR STRAUS GIROUX

New York

Text copyright © 1976, 1980 by Richard Carlyon
Illustrations copyright © 1976 by Pauline Ellison
All rights reserved
First American edition, 1980
Printed in the United States of America
Designed by Irving Perkins

Library of Congress Cataloging in Publication Data
Carlyon, Richard.
The dark Lord of Pengersick.
SUMMARY: Mabby and Jago determine to defeat the
Lord of Pengersick, an evil sorcerer who has filled the
lives of the people of the surrounding area with misery
and terror.
[1.   Fantasy]   I.   Title.
PZ7.C2169Dar   1980   [Fic]   80-13360
ISBN 0-374-31700-3

For Leo Benedict,
who saw it happen

Kenidjack

Mulfra

Pensans

Pen an
Wlas

Boscawen

Kemy

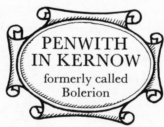

PENWITH
IN KERNOW
formerly called
Bolerion

Bretan Vyghan

Ywerdhon

Porth Ia

Caer an Dinas

Dyndajel

utral

Bosvenegh

Marghas Yow

Polcrebo Downs

k los

Bal Dhu   Godolphin

Pencaire

Trenoweth

Keneggy Downs   Germoe

Pengersick

Gudden   Breage

Prah Sands

Gweek

Lesart   Polkimbro

THE DARK LORD
OF PENGERSICK

1

Pengersick Tower

A long time ago on the coast of Kernow, before the beginning of almost everything else, a tower was built. In time, men came to call it the Dark Tower of Pengersick, for it was built of the dark moorland granite, far from the eyes of all honest men, at the head of a marsh.

Men whispered that it was built by the Lord of Pengersick, newly returned from wanderings in the East. But none could swear to that, for many years had passed since the young Pengersick had left the valley to journey overseas. None could swear that it was indeed he, for all they saw was a cloaked figure in the distance, pacing out the ground with thoughtful strides or standing staring at the sea from under a ragged tree, while the wind whipped the waves until they moaned in pain.

The observers noticed that in rough weather the distant figure seemed larger and more active than at other times. It was as if the cloaked man drew strength from the torment of the elements.

Not long after his arrival, the crofters and fishermen found that all their accustomed paths across the lands belonging to the manor of Pengersick had been blocked by barriers made of thorns and sharpened staves. They had to find other ways down to the sea.

One way only remained unblocked, the ancient track that ran to the sea down a little zawn. The zawn was said to be the royal highway of the small people, the original spirits of the earth, and men kept a respectful distance between themselves and it. There was one family, named Trenoweth, who used the way unhindered; legend held that the first Trenoweth had done the small ones a favor. Thus the family, though desperately poor, had always survived, and even now were living in their ancestral cottage at the head of the zawn.

One day a deep rumbling noise was heard descending from the ridge. Men came running for an explanation: the farmers from their fields, the tinners from their streams, the merchants from their counters. All came running to see the long procession of heavy carts and wagons, which creaked and jolted on the road down to Pengersick.

The carts were loaded with timber, ropes, and all the implements of the mason's trade. The wagons were piled with blocks of fresh-cut stone and great vats of quicklime and mortar. And the men, whipping at the oxen, trudging by the wheels, sitting on the bouncing tailboards, were swarthy and bright-eyed. They ignored the country people, speaking softly to each other, and to the oxen, in a strange singing language that had something of the mountains in it. They showed no interest, betrayed no curiosity.

The procession reached the lands of Pengersick and disappeared behind the barriers of thorn. But from a nearby hill the inquisitive inhabitants continued to watch.

The strangers began work that very day, digging, hauling, cutting, mixing, fixing, hammering, and chiseling. They worked with solid determination, with few words and no songs. They worked all day, and then far into the night by the aromatic light of pine flares. They even worked upon holy days and days of rest, rudely ignoring the customs of the land. When the elders tried to object, the strangers tied fierce dogs to the hedges and boundary posts around the lord's estates, and they patrolled with slings and billhooks.

At last the tower was finished, its grim battlements rising from a protective group of mighty pine trees, its thin blank windows staring like empty eye sockets in a skull. About the tower were stables and lodgings for animals and men; there was a small gatehouse, and a huge oaken door studded with iron nails. The whole place was encircled by a simple earth bank and ditch, designed more for baffling straying cattle than for keeping out determined foes.

Before they left, the masons held a strange ritual, accompanied by deep unearthly chanting. Then they pulled down their lodges and made a great heap of all their ropes, tools, devices, and spare timber—even the wagons. They set fire to the pile, and as it crackled and blazed, they slaughtered sufficient oxen for a seven days' feast. At the end of that time, they dragged their one remaining ox to the top of a nearby hill and sacrificed it there. They nailed its dripping skull and wide horns to a tree as a sign of their passing. And then they walked away, as abruptly as they had come.

The savage dogs were withdrawn to the kennels, and soon smiling men came overland from the north coast, from Ywerdhon, with strings of horses for the Pengersick stables. The horse traders were a noisy lot, and the inn on the road did good trade. But if anyone asked any questions about Pengersick, the traders would wink broadly, shake their heads, and order more ale.

The horse traders left one of their number in the tower, a tall man who seemed to have taken on the job of steward of the estates. He rode about the countryside recruiting young men to be servants and huntsmen. He seemed to choose only the good-for-nothings, the layabouts and bully boys, and he paid them well, so well that they never visited their families; not that that was too great a loss. Anyone who succumbed to the lure of the steward's gold was mourned as dead by his friends, for all those who took up employment seemed to change, to begin to live apart, to become as strangers.

Now began an evil time, for Pengersick's ruffians took eagerly to their tasks of looting and terrorizing the unhappy land. Nothing was safe. They would take the offerings at a holy shrine, a fisherman's catch, a widow's solitary cow—not for their small value, but for the distress their loss would cause. Heavier taxes were imposed, duties on every article needed to sustain life were increased, and what they could not get legally, they took anyway, for there was no law now but boot and whip. Those who complained were summarily hauled off to the tower. One youth who dared raise his hand against Pengersick had that hand struck off.

The people turned for help to the race of small folk, variously known as elves, or piskies, or spriggans. But these small people were also struggling against the Lord. Their ancient powers had grown weak; Pengersick's gold had found traitors among them, and had turned their talents as miners to his own advantage. He had forced them into virtual slavery, a thing that made the ordinary folk shudder, for they held the little people in great esteem and awe.

People began to move away from Pengersick. Land in the valley became cheap, and the fishing boats on the wide sands of Prah became less numerous. For it was hinted that the Lord of Pengersick had uncanny evil in his dark eyes—that he was a sorcerer.

The Dark Lord, as he came to be called, was seen seldom, and then only at a distance, almost always on a black stallion. In winter, with a wild black cloak and hood pulled down low over his eyes, his flying figure resembled that of a monstrous crow. On his gloved finger he wore a ring of marvelous craft: a heavy gold ring set with a fiery black stone in the shape of a pentacle, or five-pointed star. The people called the ring the Black Sigil of Pengersick and declared that it was proof that the Lord of Pengersick was in league with the Evil One himself.

2

The Hunted Doe

Not very far from Pengersick's door, but outside his domain, on the small zawn lived the Trenoweths. There were three of them living in the cottage: Father Trenoweth; Mother Trenoweth, lame and ill; and the child of their old age, Mabby (or as they called her in their Kernewek speech, Mabby-vean, which means "little Mabby"). The old couple had had a hard, sad life of unceasing work. Their two oldest children had left home some years before, driven away by the poverty of the land. For a while Mabby had been a lady's maid, a great favorite of the Lady of Germoe, who had taught her to read and write, but she had returned home to care for her aging parents.

Though the other farmers and peasants avoided them because they lived in the zawn, the Trenoweths had heard of the evil ways of the Dark Lord. Jago, an orphan boy who lived among the ponies of the moor, frequently visited them, and he knew the comings and goings of all the folk in that part of Kernow. Unlike many of their neighbors, it never occurred to them to leave. The little farm was theirs. Had not Trenoweths lived there from before recorded time, working their stony fields? Were they not under the special protection of the small folk? Were they not the only people allowed to use the zawn unhindered? And was not the free, wild moor—a way of escape in need— but a short scramble up the hill?

One day, as Mabby was hoeing their field, she heard the

distant clamor of hunting dogs in full cry. Moments later, a young doe, all lathered with sweat and panting fit to die, leaped over the stone wall and collapsed in the field, exhausted.

As quickly as she could, Mabby snatched up her cloak and covered the animal with it. But the cloak, which was her only covering against wind and rain, was badly tattered. There was one large hole in particular through which the doe's soft hide was clearly visible.

Mabby took the crust of bread that was her food for the day and covered the hole with it. The doe, realizing the danger, lay absolutely still: so still that from a distance the bread looked as if it had been placed on a rock.

The fearful yelping grew louder and nearer, until it clamored bloodthirstily on the other side of the mossy gate. The dogs, sensing a power in the Trenoweth field they had not encountered before, sniffed the air and refused to leap over the gate. The huntsmen shouted and cracked their whips, but the hounds stayed where they were.

One of the huntsmen came forward and placed his hand on the gate. But as he did so, a quiet, faraway look came into his eyes. His hand fell to his side and he seemed unable to go on. The other huntsmen yelled louder and whipped the dogs, until blood sprayed onto the ground.

Mabby watched in horror the treatment of the hounds; but she remembered the doe and knew that the dogs would not hesitate to tear her apart if they had the chance.

Suddenly, all fell silent. The huntsmen stepped aside fearfully as a tall figure rode forward. It could be none other than the sorcerer himself, the Dark Lord of Pengersick.

Mabby shivered with fear. Then she thought of the poor doe and was angry once more. The man drew up his horse and looked down at her scornfully.

"Why?" he hissed. "Why do you stand in my way, girl?" Mabby was too scared to reply.

"Where is my quarry? Answer me. Where is the doe?" Still Mabby did not answer.

"Do you know who I am?"

"You are the Lord of Pengersick," said Mabby, her voice trembling. "But you are no lord here. We are free farmers, and these are the fields of the Trenoweths. We owe our allegiance only to the Earl, and you will have to answer to him when he returns if you harm us. You may not enter here."

The sorcerer looked surprised. He raised his hand and uncovered his head. Mabby saw a mop of unruly black hair, black gleaming eyes, and red lips set in a black beard.

"A long speech from one so short. I ask you again, have you seen my doe?"

Mabby refused to speak. The sorcerer grew impatient.

"Reply, or it will be the worse for you!" he said, and his keen eyes searched the field. He moved forward, but was met by a force he did not recognize. Then he realized its source and smiled sarcastically.

He shouted for his men and dogs to leave, to return to Pengersick. But before he wheeled his own horse about, the sorcerer shook his hand free and casually pointed his ring at the shape in the field: the cloak with the bit of bread on it.

He shouted a strange word. There was a sharp crack and a flash of blue flame broke from his ring and spread through the air at the cloak. Startled, Mabby fell to the ground. The field was filled with the smell of burning.

The Dark Lord laughed, and spurred his horse away down the lane.

3

Help

As soon as he was out of sight, Mabby picked herself up and rushed to where the doe was hidden. The evil fire had charred the edge of the garment, but to her relief the doe was unhurt. She hugged the animal delightedly. She realized that the sorcerer's attack had been for show, to impress his power on her and his men; he had not used the force he was capable of.

She looked tenderly at the doe. "Well, my beautiful one, what are we to do with you now? If you go off by yourself, those dogs will kill you, for sure."

Mabby thought hard. It obviously amused the sorcerer to play with her like this, to frighten her. But now she had a respite, a chance to do something to save the doe. She must not waste the opportunity. On the other side of the valley there lived a kind old man, a hermit. No one ever went there, so the doe would be quite safe with him.

Mabby fastened the now burned and ragged cloak about her and led the way. Quietly the two of them slipped into the shadow of the thorn brakes. They went by way of sunken roads used only by smugglers, and across patches of gorse where the wind sang rustily, until they came to the place where the hermit lived.

The hermit's bothy leaned against the wide trunk of an ancient oak tree. It seemed to be part of the oak; its outer covering had merged with the bark of the tree, and the branches

10

of the tree had grown across the hut, strengthening it. It was difficult to see which was tree and which was hut. In front was a herb garden, growing in natural disarray, and from the nearby bushes hung a living net of tangled creepers.

The hard winds that blew in from the sea and moorland lost their way among the trees, shrubs, and rocks of the hermit's domain, and only a few gentle streams of air survived to fill the place with the fragrance of herbs and flowers.

In the little disordered garden Mabby could recognize sea aster, scurvy grass, hedge bedstraw, celandine, rhubarb, spleenwort, golden saxifrage, hemlock, whortleberry, sorrel, campion, burdock, toadflax and pellitory, polypody and buckthorn, mustard and betony, poppy and lavender. The more she looked, the more she saw, until she ran out of names. Mabby knew that every plant had some use, good or evil, common or obscure; and it seemed to her that every plant was here in the garden.

She walked toward the little bothy and smiled nervously as she noticed the hermit standing in the doorway. He wore a simple tunic and leggings; his tanned brow was wrinkled, and his long, thin fingers held a small bundle of twigs, tied together with straw.

He looked at Mabby and immediately she felt at ease. She sensed that he knew about her and the doe.

They went inside. The interior smelled of all the seasons, mixed with wood smoke. Herbs, flowers, leaves, roots, aromatic barks, and bunches of twigs hung from the walls and roof. Birds fluttered down to the open window to peck at the sprinkling of grain on the ledge, and a group of small furry woodland creatures lazed in the cold hearth.

"Don't worry, child," said the hermit. "I'm glad you came to me so soon. I was expecting you."

"How?" asked Mabby, somehow not really surprised.

The hermit smiled and pointed to the birds pecking at the grain.

"I have friends everywhere. Now let the poor doe come in. I have something that can help her."

Mabby led the doe into the hut. The hermit said a few quiet words, which the animal appeared to understand. He took a stone vessel from the shelf and poured some dark liquid into a wooden bowl. The doe drank.

"It may seem hard to understand, girl, but this drink will make the doe safe from the huntsmen. It will make her invisible until she regains her strength."

As Mabby watched, the doe seemed to get fainter and fainter, as if evaporating. The hermit smiled.

"It's not black witchcraft," he said. "All I've done is rearrange the way light is reflected from her skin. The doe's still there, as solid as ever."

Mabby nodded sadly. "Goodbye, doe. Be safe, dear one."

Although she could no longer see the doe, Mabby could hear her leaving the hut. She sat silently for a moment, then looked at the hermit.

"Sir, what can we do? Will no one fight the Dark Lord?"

The hermit sighed. He sat down on a bench and looked around at his little house.

"Child-vean, I sense things to come. There will be great trouble and pain ahead, many sad days, many terrible nights. Even the strongest will lose faith."

"I'm not strong," said Mabby, "but I'll do anything to stop that man. He's an evil sorcerer, that's plain from the way he's been able to bend everyone to his will."

"Yes, yes, he is. But who is stronger than he?"

"You are strong."

"I am old. The part I can play is small. I have spent all my life with gentle things. I know about plants and their good uses, about animals and trees, about the winds and stones and streams. My strength is dispersed, and this is not my battle. It needs someone young, active, and with enthusiasm for sharp, hectic struggles."

Mabby stared at the wooden bowl. There was still some of the potion left untouched. The thought entered her head that if she were to drink it, she, too, would become invisible. What a weapon to use against the sorcerer!

The hermit read her thoughts. He stood up and took the bowl in both hands, swirling the liquid around. It had a sharp smell.

"I will not stop you if you want to drink it. I have no right to tell anyone what to do. I am merely the guardian of these things. But, child, you in your innocence have greater strength than many with guile and cunning. Before you take up the challenge, know that you will see such terrors as no one has dreamed of, frightful sights of sorrow and sadness. You will get little help from others to start with. But help will come, that I promise you. This potion works for humans as well as animals —aye, better in a way, for humans can control its effect by will, which animals cannot do. It will enable you to enter the tower unseen. Once there, you can spy on the enchanter. Knowledge is power, and knowledge that lies in books may be carried off secretly. Be brave, Mabby Trenoweth, for all the good power of the earth, of the plants that flower overnight, of stones and streams, all these are with you. Go, be brave, use strength and you will become stronger."

Mabby hesitated. But then the memory of the doe returned, and with it came a deep determination to fight the evil man with everything in her power. She took the wooden bowl and drank the dark liquid.

"To become invisible at will, cross your fingers like this and say the word 'Tetragrammaton' three times. And three times more to revert to your former self. You can do it whenever you want to, and the power will never fade. You must go now, child, for the wind has changed direction and the moorland choughs will be flying this way. Don't let them see you, for they are a telltale lot and servants of the Dark Lord."

Mabby said goodbye to the old hermit and quickly left the hut. She ran as fast as she could back to the field to collect her hoe, before going home to the little white-walled cottage by the moor.

4

Tetragrammaton!

All that day and well into the next, Mabby thought about the events that had taken place. She knew that in the hermit's potion she had a powerful weapon, and she was eager to try it out as soon as she could.

The hours passed, and with them her resolve to fight the evil power of the sorcerer strengthened. She decided to wait no longer; she would visit the enchanter's castle tonight.

Mabby's eyes were bright with excitement as she got up and put on her dress, clogs, and shawl. Then she took the clogs off again, for they would make too much noise.

She crossed her fingers tightly and took a deep breath. Slowly she said the word "Tetragrammaton" three times.

Nothing happened. Mabby wondered if she had said the word correctly. It was a difficult one to remember, and it had to be exactly right for the potion to work. She turned to her small mirror, and with a thrill realized that there was no reflection!

Yet, looking down, she could see her hands, body, and legs perfectly; she could count all her toes one by one. She was invisible, not to herself, but to others.

Out of the cottage she went, swiftly and silently. She climbed the slope out of the zawn and met the main track that led to the boundaries of Pengersick.

She heard voices and noticed three figures coming toward her. They were fishermen, three rascally fellows who kept the castle supplied with fish and lobster, and who used the protection of the sorcerer to indulge in other pursuits, such as smuggling.

The three of them were sharing a bottle.

"You've had your share, Treverran," bellowed one of them, as the man they called Treverran took a long swig at the bottle.

"Ach, shut up, or I'll bust your head," growled Treverran.

"Quiet down, you two," said the third. "You'll waken the spirits."

"Spirits! What spirits? Miserable little gnomes more like, groveling for a crumb or a free drink of milk out of the cat's saucer. I'll have no truck with any of them."

"Hush, man. Who knows what creatures the sorcerer has in his power. The very stones will tell on you. Oww!"

The speaker stopped in horror, for a stone had nudged his elbow and plunked at his feet.

"What's up? Give us the bottle," said one of his companions.

"Preserve us, did you see that?" said the other man.

"Whaaaa . . . ?"

The bottle seemed to pull itself out of Treverran's hand. It floated in the air in front of the astounded trio. Then it up-ended itself, and the drink flooded out onto the roadway.

With a great wail of fear the three men backed off; then they turned and ran for their lives, as if all the demons of the pit were after them with burning sulfur.

Mabby laughed, and at the silvery tinkle of sound the men ran even faster. She left the bottle standing in the middle of the road with a stone balanced on top, and walked almost cheerfully in the direction of Pengersick Tower.

The place looked forbidding. Within earshot of the sea, the square keep jutted up from wind-swept trees, alive with dark birds. The long, low bank was broken by a single gate, although here and there it had been holed by fallen trees and sliding earth. Peering over the bank, Mabby could see lights gleaming from the group of smaller buildings surrounding the castle. She could hear the clank of metal being worked at; the puff-clang of the forge, where even at this late hour chains were being fashioned for the feet of some poor captive. And over the sound of metal came the growling of savage dogs, fighting over scraps of food.

The night birds set up a caw-cawing as they sensed an alien presence. Their shrill noise reached the ears of the sorcerer, whose acute hearing missed nothing unusual. Gruffly he ordered his servants to search the grounds and make all secure. And out they came, with snarling dogs on short chains, their blazing torches lighting up the damp tree trunks.

They searched and found nothing. Sullenly, they returned to the castle and gave the all-clear.

Mabby ran through the trees and caught up with the last man. He walked with a limp, jingling a large bunch of keys at his leather belt.

Mabby guessed he must be the porter. She made a quick decision and followed him. As he went through the narrow gap in the oak door, she squeezed in behind.

With a rusty screech and a hollow thud, the great door of the castle closed firmly behind her. She was inside the dreaded tower of Pengersick.

5

Inside the Tower

Mabby's feet were suddenly cold from the cobbles, and a nearby crash of chains and outburst of furious barking made her jump with fear. She nearly pitched into the porter, who had stopped at the gratings behind which the dogs leaped and growled.

Cursing them for being so noisy, the porter picked up a large stone and flung it at the dogs, making them cower and whimper. Then he went on his way. Mabby gave a shiver and followed him. They went past stables, heavy with the smell of horses, and into the innermost part of the tower.

There was a door into a bright, noisy guardroom. The porter looked in and took a copper jug from a hook, winking at the guards, who were rolling dice on the top of a dirty table. Mabby followed him along a dingy corridor into a huge kitchen, where a few stupid-looking louts were cleaning dirty pots and licking at crusts of gray bread, soaked in greasy gravy. The porter went over to an enormous wooden barrel supported on wedges. He bent down and twirled the spigot, causing a stream of dark wine to froth into the copper jug.

Mabby took a good look at the kitchen. There were long shelves piled with food of all kinds; hams and fat sausages hung from the rafters; there were sides of cured bacon, great tubs of salted fish and pork, a tank full of live lobsters, barrels of flour and grain, jars of preserved meats and fruits, sacks of vegetables,

18

and nets of oysters. There were glass pots full of costly spices and, above them, great round cheeses, bottles of spirits, and jugs of cider.

Mabby had never seen so many good things in one place before. She thought of her parents' store, which contained half a dozen salted pilchards and a small bag of coarse flour.

Then she noticed a cluster of game birds hanging by their feet, their necks flapping and their eyes glassy. The sight of them, so cruelly trussed, filled Mabby with pity and anger.

She turned her attention back to the porter. He had filled two jugs with wine; one was the battered copper vessel he had taken from the guardroom, the other was of finely decorated silver, with an ornate handle.

Mabby noticed it with excitement: surely it must be intended for the sorcerer himself. To get to him, she had only to follow the porter.

The porter took both jugs and left the kitchen, with Mabby in invisible pursuit. As he climbed the staircase, he stopped for a moment to hide the copper jug, which was for himself, in a corner.

The higher they went, the wider and better lit the stairs became, until they arrived at a landing with richly paneled walls hung with beautiful tapestries. The porter halted in front of a door, tapped, and waited. From the other side a bell tinkled; the porter opened the door.

Mabby gasped. She had never seen anything so rich and fine. To her the room was like a dream. Light from the fire was added to by four tall lamps. The walls were draped with damask and lined with books and strange pictures. The marble floor had curious mosaic designs, which could be seen between the scattered fur rugs.

The sorcerer himself was there; he did not look up. He sat in a huge carved chair, his black-bearded chin sunk in his cupped hand. He was dressed in a silk tunic and had a bear fur around his shoulders. His eyes gazed broodingly ahead, at nothing in particular.

The porter carefully put the silver jug of wine on the ivory-inlaid table, and left the room.

Mabby remained by the door, motionless. She was a little frightened by the room, of its strange furnishings, and of the dark, somber man slumped in the chair. She remembered the stories that Jago, the pony boy, had brought with him across the wild moor, stories he had heard of this place, of its dungeons and prisoners, and tales of the sorcerer dancing on the battlements at midnight with a whirling crowd of demons.

In front of the sorcerer was a candle that burned with a steady upright flame. By its light, Mabby noticed, on the window ledge beyond, a small book bound with hairy gray skin. Perhaps it contained some clue to the sorcerer's power. Perhaps his spells could be learned from it.

She went over to the book and stealthily began to turn the heavy pages, one by one. The words were written in crabbed and difficult hand, though here and there she recognized a familiar word. The drawings were strange and incomprehensible.

The sorcerer shivered and pulled the bear fur closer around his shoulders. He poured some wine from the jug into a tall crystal goblet. As he did so, he noticed a movement reflected in the crystal: the movement of the heavy vellum pages. Strange, no draft had ever moved the pages like that.

A suspicion crept into his mind; his quick brain considered the possibilities. Then he closed his eyes and pretended to doze.

After a while, he felt a cold draft by his side, as if someone had passed by. He opened one eye very slowly and was surprised to feel a warm sensation on his little finger. He looked at it through his lashes: his hand lay lightly on the carved armrest of the chair. He saw the five-pointed ring, the Black Sigil of Pengersick, move slightly, slide down his finger, come off, and then rise gently into the air. It moved away, quite fast, toward the door, as if it were being carried.

What power dared to challenge him here at the very center of his stronghold? He almost smiled at the audacity of the act. Then, swiftly, his thoughts changed. He would find out who presumed so much. Whoever it was would be allowed a long, long rope, long enough to lead him to the source of this impudence—and then that person would feel his power.

The sorcerer waited until the ring was out of sight. Silently he slipped out of the chair and ran to the door.

The shining gold metal was easy to spot in the dark; he followed the ring along the gallery and down the stairs, making no attempt to raise the alarm. Whatever the mystery was, he intended to get to the bottom of it himself.

Soon they were out among the trees. The ring went faster now, straight for the wall, and finding a section where the bank was broken, it glided through. Mabby knew she was being followed, but there seemed to be no way to hide the ring. She could not make it invisible to Pengersick but she could not bear to give it up. With the ring securely on her finger, she rushed across the road and hid behind a bush.

A black figure vaulted noiselessly over the bank and landed in a crouching position, his bright eyes searching the darkness. She headed up the road toward her home at top speed. Although she was invisible, she could not go faster than normal, and it seemed to her that her pursuer was gaining ground with every stride.

Suddenly Mabby realized that the sorcerer had no intention of merely catching up with her. He wanted to follow her back to wherever she had come from. That meant he didn't know who she was, or where she was headed. A counter-plan formed in her mind. She left the road and went down a small pathway overhung with branches and deeply carpeted with thick grass.

The way got narrower and wilder. Briers caught at the

sorcerer's clothes, forcing him to go more slowly. But Mabby, being small and nimble, was able to evade them easily.

She ran on, aware that just around the corner was a junction, a confusing interlacing of thin paths.

The sorcerer found it difficult to keep up. He was unused to walking in rough country; usually he rode everywhere. He saw the ring disappear around a bend and shouted to himself in silent anger, as a thick bramble clutched at his leg.

By the time he was free and around the corner, the ring was nowhere to be seen.

The enchanter looked about him. The maze of bushes, shrubs, hedges, briers, and rocks had no outstanding characteristics that would lead him back to this spot. Although still not far from his castle, he had never been here before, and there must be dozens of such forks in the wild paths that ran around the countryside.

He had an idea. He took out a sharp knife and cut off a thin branch from a bush. He stripped it of leaves and bark, sharpened it, and stuck it securely into the ground alongside the path, just before the fork. He put it where its thin white shape could easily be seen by someone searching for it, but not so close to the path that any passing cow or peasant could knock it over.

He intended to return the next morning with a gang of trackers and huntsmen. The shaved branch would tell them where to begin their search, and in a short time they would recover the ring and capture the thief. He looked forward to having such a bold fellow in his dungeons. Smiling cruelly in anticipation, he strolled back to his castle.

Mabby ran homeward in fear and trembling. She knew that the ring was of immense value to the Lord, so why had he risked letting it out of his sight?

She stopped before the little white cottage, wondering where she could hide the ring. Certainly not at home, for she could well imagine what terrible revenge the sorcerer would take upon her parents if it was found there. She thought hard, and then remembered the cave at Gwynmaen. Just outside the boundary of her father's land, it was in a wild jumble of briers, gorse, and gigantic boulders. The ring would be safe there.

Mabby hurried to the cave, skillfully negotiating her way behind the screen of thorns and bushes. Inside, undisturbed, she found some things she had left last summer: candle ends, an old box, and some rags. She lifted the lid of the box and put the ring inside, first carefully wrapping it in rags.

Then she left.

6

The Dark Lord Goes Hunting

It was morning. The clouds moved away from the sea and sailed high over the valleys and fields until they skimmed the topmost pinnacles of Castel an Dinas to the west, and Pencaire, Tregonning, and Godolphin to the east. The sun came to warm the long sands of Prah, and to glint on the waves that covered the sunken cities of Hernyetis and Mountamopus. There, below the ice-cold waters, lay ruined walls and fallen towers. When the sea rushed and foamed at the rocks in its winter rage, it was said that you could hear voices in harmonious chants— the voices of the drowned people who were at prayer when the flood burst in upon them. After a storm the fishermen, snug behind their stone walls and oak doors, could hear the distant clang of a ghostly underwater bell.

Mabby remembered these stories of ancient Lyonesse whenever she rested at the top of the zawn, in sight of the sea. Today the sea was peaceful, and nothing but the distant cry of the gulls and the gentle hiss of a soft wind among the thorns could be heard.

She picked up her long-handled hoe and began to work. The sun was still quite low, but it had already made short work of the morning mists.

From the valley of Pengersick came a chilling sound: the snort of horses and the clink of their iron shoes aclatter on the cobbled courtyard. Mabby ran to the stone hedge and saw, a

24

mile and more below her, a small group of horses leaving the shelter of the trees about the grim stronghold. It was the Lord of Pengersick and his men.

But the sight did not alarm Mabby. She knew that the sorcerer had followed her last night, but since then there had been a heavy dew; even the best tracking dogs would find it impossible to trace her steps.

The Lord of Pengersick rode out of his castle in a determined mood. The day was bright; he had slept soundly in spite of the evening's loss, and had breakfasted well on venison and cream. He intended to retrace his steps and discover the path he had marked with the stripped stick. Then he would find the person who had had the impudence to purloin his ring. And punish him.

He had realized from the unusual way the ring had left him that magic was involved, but he was certain that his own magic was far stronger than that of any country-bred Kernow peasant. Yet he was interested in meeting the thief. He wanted to know what sort of person would take such a mad risk; surely everyone knew how powerful he was?

The Dark Lord and his men left the road and went up the little ride. Soon the way became too narrow and overgrown for their horses. Forced to dismount, they left the animals with a groom and set off on foot.

The sun blazed down on them, and they were soon puffing and sweating. Their heavy boots with spurs were fine protection against the trailing briers, but were not at all easy to walk in. One of the men tripped and pitched sideways into a gully lined with spiky coils of bramble. The others hooted with laughter. They left him there to fend for himself and pushed onward.

The trail never seemed to end. It grew narrower and more difficult, until they reached a part where the sun had not penetrated and the ground underfoot was squelchy with mud.

At last they came to a fork in the path.

"Which way do we take, my lord?" asked one of them gruffly.

"Look just off the path for a switch I cut and stripped the bark off. That marks where I last saw the ring."

They searched, but without success.

"Blast me if I can see it," muttered one man to his friend.

"Go on looking, fellow, else you'll get his lordship's whip across your rump," whispered the other.

"Well?" said the sorcerer. "Have you idiots eyes in your thick heads or not? Ach, let *me* have a look, then."

As he looked he became perplexed, for search as he would he could see no sign of the shaved stick he had placed so carefully.

"This cannot be the right fork," he muttered. "Let's go on."

"But . . . which way?" asked one of the trackers.

"What do you think, dunderpoll! Both ways, of course! We'll split forces. The first to find the stick gives two blasts on the horn. Let's get on with it."

After hours spent walking in circles searching for the stick, the sorcerer's men were scratched and bruised, their faces stung by insects, their hands roughened by thorns. They were hot and thirsty, footsore and weary, and mightily fed up.

Had they known the truth, they would have screamed in frustration. For by some strange power of nature the stick they were looking for had taken root overnight. It had grown bark, budded, and put forth small branches and fresh green leaves. It stood where it had been planted, but now it was impossible to distinguish from the hundreds of others around it. The things of the earth, the plants and stones, followed a more ancient power than the sorcerer's: the power of the earth itself.

The Dark Lord was in a towering rage, for he realized that an unexpected kind of magic had been at work—magic about which he knew nothing. He had been made to look a fool. He had failed to recover his ring.

Without waiting for the others, he stamped back to where

they had left the horses. He rode furiously to the castle, whipping his stallion until its foaming sweat was marked with drops of dark red blood.

It was not until that afternoon that the people of Penwith were to learn the full extent of the sorcerer's fury. Then troops of grim-faced horsemen rode about the country with swords at their sides and coils of strong rope at their saddles. By late afternoon the sorcerer had rounded up anyone who had a reputation for dealing in the magic arts: every warlock, every wizard, every old woman who sold love potions to young plowmen, every fortuneteller from the coast, everyone who cast runes, or scried into crystal, or read cards. From Sennar to Landewednack, from Pensans to Germoe, from Ludgvan to Kerthen, they all came into the castle, bound hand and foot.

Then the sorcerer's men went out again into the countryside with a demand that everyone should attend at the cliff of Cudden the following noon, on pain of death.

They all gathered, just before noon, on a grassy plot not far from the edge of the fearful cliff. Two hundred feet below them the surf pounded on sharp black rocks.

Soon a procession approached. It was led by the sorcerer himself, the hood of his cloak pulled down low over his cruel eyes. Behind him rode his men, clad in iron and leather, guarding a group of captives. The latter presented a sorry spectacle. Their clothing was torn, and some had black eyes and dried blood about their faces.

Mabby, who was standing in the crowd, searched in vain for the gentle features of the hermit.

The sorcerer reined in his horse and sat glaring at the silent people. It was his steward who spoke.

"People of Penwith: let it be known that my Lord of Pengersick has suffered a grievous hurt. A felony has been committed. And that by magic, by foul magic!"

The crowd remained silent. They knew full well that Pengersick himself was in league with the devil, but no one had the courage to object to the outrageous accusation.

"Now let it be known that a valuable ring, the Sigil of Pengersick, has been stolen . . ."

A cry of amazement burst from the throng. Who could have been so brave, so foolish as to steal the famous ring?

". . . and the thief used magic arts for his crime. Here before you are those who are known to use unnatural arts, sorcery, witchcraft, and the like. None of them will confess. Something is being hidden."

He stepped forward and, drawing his dagger, plunged it into the earth. Then he placed his glove on the grass, not far from the shadow of the dagger.

"You have until the shadow reaches the glove. If nothing is revealed by then . . . well, these evildoers will suffer the punishment they deserve."

He stepped back and folded his arms. A whispering broke out among the crowd: a ferment of worry, suspicion, and terror.

Mabby hid her face. She could not bear to watch. She had heard the hermit's warning, but she had never thought that by struggling against the sorcerer she would endanger the lives of others, the lives of innocent people. Yet the hermit had said that someone would come to help her. She took a deep breath. She would count to three, then she would step forward and confess. She couldn't let those people die. She began counting: "One, two . . ." Suddenly she felt a gentle hand on her shoulder, and whirled around. "Jago!"

"Mabby."

Jago, a smiling lad, with a mop of unruly black hair, lived alone on the moors, where he tamed and traded moorland ponies. He himself was untamable: a wild, kind, careless creature who preferred his freedom above his comfort. And so

he was very poor, but also very happy. Mabby noticed he led his favorite pony, Ligger, on a rope.

"Now then, Mabby, don't cry. You're a Trenoweth. I know things look bad, but we'll be fine, right enough."

The shadow crept on.

Now the only sound was the mewing of the gulls and the slap-slap-slap of the surf. Still the shadow crept on, until it was only the width of a sword from the edge of the glove. The sorcerer took his hand out of his cloak and was about to raise it.

"Hold on there."

A ripple of relief ran through the crowd. They looked around to see who had shouted. It was Jago. He now sat at the back of the throng on his pony. He wore a sheepskin jerkin and tattered breeches that stopped at the knee; from there to his brown feet, his legs were bare. His pony had no saddle or bridle, only a rope and a wooden bit.

"Come forward, lad, so we can see you," shouted the steward.

"I'm fine where I am, thank you," replied Jago. At this the sorcerer looked up at him, and those in front of Jago quailed at his fiery glare. They gradually pressed themselves back, leaving a gap in the crowd.

"What do you have to say?" asked the steward.

"How much will I get if I tell you where I last saw the ring?" asked Jago.

"Describe the ring first, young man."

"It's solid gold and it's got a black stone. The stone is shaped like a five-point star. On either side of the star the ring is shaped like a serpent's head. One serpent has its mouth closed, the other shows its fangs."

The Lord of Pengersick turned his head quickly in interest. From his glove he drew a coin, a fat, gold coin that shone like the sun. Silently he tossed it through the air toward Jago.

Jago twitched his bare foot against the pony's side. The

animal altered its position slightly, and Jago caught the coin without seeming to notice it. He calmly pushed it into his belt.

"Now, young man, earn that coin," yelled the steward.

"Sir, I saw the ring in someone's possession very recently."

There was a murmur of disapproval from the crowd. Although they felt relieved, they could not stomach the thought of a betrayal. Some who did not know Jago hissed at him and raised their fists in anger.

"I saw the ring on a man's finger as he rode past me. I was on Keneggy Downs by the leech pool."

"When was this? Who was the man?"

"It was two days ago, and the man was mounted on a black horse. He was accompanied by a lot of fat-faced, treacherous louts, and he wore a black cloak. In fact it was your companion there, the fellow who's so generous with his gold."

And he pointed with his stained finger straight at the Dark Lord.

A cry of delighted laughter went up from the crowd, for Jago had given nothing away. He had simply said that the last time he had seen the ring was on the sorcerer's finger. He had not claimed to have seen the ring *since* its theft.

The sorcerer's men dashed forward angrily, but the boy on his little pony was too swift. He galloped off at breakneck speed, hooting with triumph.

"After him," screamed the steward.

But the Dark Lord shook his head and with a careful gesture raised his fist.

"Oh no, the poor lad!" cried out a woman from the crowd. The people watched, fascinated, but unable to help Jago. They found they could not even call a warning.

The sorcerer rose in his saddle. With narrowed eyes he stared at the fleeing figure of Jago. Then, suddenly, he pointed in his direction, as if throwing a spear. At the same time he shouted out a strange and dreadful word.

Open-mouthed, the assembled people saw a great sheet of fire burst all around the boy and his pony. The animal bucked in fear, then slithered sideways, taking the boy with him.

Boy and pony struggled hopelessly as a covering of brambles gave way, and a black hole appeared beneath it. The pony gave a last neigh of terror as the two of them disappeared.

There was a silence, followed by a dreadful noise: a hollow, echoing noise, as bone and flesh hit solid rock, scores of feet below. Then silence once again.

"Let no one attempt to rescue him," said the steward sternly.

The Dark Lord looked at him without speaking, then rode off toward Pengersick.

The captives turned toward the steward fearfully.

"My master has made up his mind to rid our fair land of all evil magic arts. You are all self-confessed wizards, warlocks, witches, pellars, and spell-binders. But my master is merciful. Your lives will be spared for now, but if the ring is not found, you will pay the price. Every three months, one of you will be brought here and cast over the cliff, until the ring is found. Go now, and do all you can to find it."

Mabby was still in a state of shock after the dreadful fate that had befallen Jago. She knew that if she had given up the ring, none of this would have happened. But she had made up her mind and was going to stick to her decision. She trusted in Jago. She felt that, like the doe, he was under the strong protection of the countryside. The earth itself seemed to give him strength. Sadly, she returned home.

7

Jago in the Pit

Jago moaned and woke up. He felt a soft, heavy weight on his leg. He tried to move it, but as he did so a spasm of pain shot up to his knee. He gasped and blinked his eyes.

He stared about him, trying to see in the gloom. He wondered where he was and how he had got there.

Suddenly it all came back: the meeting on the cliff top, the prisoners and soldiers, the Lord of Pengersick and the ring.

But where was he? Where was his pony, Ligger? He remembered that as he had ridden away a sheet of flame had burst from the ground; his pony had reared and they had both fallen into blackness.

He looked up. Far above his head he could see a circular area of deeper dark, sprinkled with gleaming stars . . . the night sky.

He was in a mine of some kind. Dark galleries spread out from the place where he lay, and the sides of the shaft were sheer and hard.

He felt something sticky on his leg. It was blood. He tried to move again and realized that the weight on his leg was his pony. Fear clutched at his throat.

"Hey, Ligger, Ligger lad. Up, boy, get up!"

Nothing. Grief made his eyes smart, his throat became dry. He did not want to admit it, but his pony was dead.

"You wait, Ligger boy, just let me get out of this. I'll soon get some help . . ."

Slowly Jago managed to extract his bruised limb. It was very painful, and when he tried to stand up the pain exploded up his leg. Despite himself he cried out. He screwed up his mouth into a grimace.

"Now then, Jago," he said to himself. "Grown lad like you . . . be brave. Try and stand up, find a way out of this place."

As he talked to himself, he felt his leg with his fingertips and found the place where the skin was bruised and tender.

All of a sudden he stopped talking.

"What was that?" he thought. "Sounded like voices, like feet walking along stone passages. What can it be?"

He crouched low, as if that would protect him in the gloom, and listened carefully. Yes, there it was again, a soft chattering, a gentle pattering—like a crowd of inquisitive squirrels.

Jago felt in his belt for his knife with the cherry-wood haft. He had heard all sorts of stories about mine creatures, and although he was disabled, he was determined to put up a stiff fight before they got him.

Then he saw the lights: little dancing pinpricks the color of fresh butter. They emerged from one of the tunnels and collected in a corner of the shaft.

Under the combined glow of the tiny lanterns (for that was what the lights were) he saw a curious and distressing sight. Small figures stood about in tired attitudes; some sat exhausted, others attended to bodies lying on stretchers. For a moment Jago was awestruck. He had heard of the small folk all his life, but he had never seen them before. Then he noticed that nearly all the little people were wounded in some way. There was a twittering of alarm as they spied him lying by the crushed body of the pony.

Their leader came forward with two guards in shining helmets and looked critically at Jago.

"Stars and shadows, friend," he said, in the greeting of his people.

"Stars and shadows," replied Jago. He knew that "Stars and shadows" was short for "Stars and shadows guide your eyes." Some small folk said, "Guide your eyes" or just "Your eyes," but you could say that only to a close friend.

The leader waved his hand over his shoulder in a despairing gesture.

"We're not in very good shape, I'm afraid. Anyway, welcome to our world. How are things above?"

"Not well," said Jago.

"Uh-huh, same trouble up above as down here, eh? He's getting at you too, is he? Well, some of us have had enough. We've each of us, soul by soul and clan by clan, taken a decision. Those that were afraid to come are still up in the mountains of Carn Brea, in Bal Dhu. We've been treated worse than slaves up there, but only a few of us are prepared to do something about it."

"Tell me your troubles, friend. My name's Jago. What's happened? Some of you look badly wounded."

"I see you have spilt blood, too, friend Jago. My name is Mungo Pygal, and these good fellows are as one with me in my struggle against the sorcerer. We've just had a little skirmish with some of his foul brood. We were well licked. Yes, I admit it. But we gave as good as we got, and we returned in good order to fight again. Arluth Dhu, the Dark Lord, has not heard the last of Mungo Pygal and his clansfolk."

Jago searched in his small leather bag that he kept at his belt. He found a hunk of salt pork and half a honeycomb wrapped in leaves.

"Look, friend Mungo, share this among your soldiers."

The little folk's eyes lit up when they saw the honeycomb. They nodded in delight, like small children, and carried the honeycomb into the light of the lanterns. Carefully, and with exact fairness, Mungo divided the honey. The little folk began to revive; they chattered and their laughter rang out like the sound of tiny silver bells.

There was a shrill word of command from Mungo, and in the time it takes a star to flash, the little folk were lined up in ranks—helmets on heads, spears on shoulders, legs planted firmly apart.

They gave three cheers for Jago, raising their slim spears in a great rippling shimmer.

Mungo Pygal stepped forward and placed a round flat stone the size of a checker before Jago. On the stone he placed an upturned helmet. The elves filed past the helmet, and each of them squeezed a drop of green liquid into it from tiny leather bottles that they carried. It was soon full. Then they marched away down one of the passages, singing loudly as they went, their armor glinting and their lanterns swinging.

"Death to Arluth Dhu!" shouted Mungo Pygal.

"Death to Arluth Dhu!" replied the elfin soldiers.

"Hey, wait, you fellows," shouted Jago desperately, as he saw them disappear. "Don't leave, help me get out of here, please."

But the mine had caught the echoes of the song, had multiplied its rhythms and increased its loudness, until the whole place boomed and clanged and shook. Jago's cries for help were drowned.

Gradually the sound died away, and all was quiet again.

Jago's gaze fell on the helmet, brimming with green liquid. It sparkled and gleamed. He was thirsty, his throat as dry as chalk. He took up the helmet and drank. The liquid tasted sweet, like mead, and made his tongue tingle.

"Ahhh, not bad, I wish I was not so . . . so . . . aaaahh!"

He gave a great yawn. A warm feeling of drowsiness crept over his body. He lay back, the rock felt as soft as a featherbed.

Days of purple clouds passed through Jago's mind. He

dreamed of riding on the moors across the wild heather of Lesart; of lying in the sun on Marghas Yow sands; of dancing on Pensans green; of eating herring in Porth Ya; of walking in Manaccan woods. Mabby, as beautiful as a princess, was with him, and there was no Dark Lord at Pengersick.

He awoke with a gasp. The dream disappeared, and he was still in the mine shaft. Sunshine flooded down. It must be midday, he thought.

He was warm and revived. His leg had stopped throbbing; he felt strong and eager. He stood up and studied his surroundings. Clearly it was impossible to climb the shaft without a rope. As for the tunnels, there were so many of them; which one should he try? His foot struck against something hard and metallic. It was the helmet from which he had drunk the liquid. Alongside it was the small stone that Mungo Pygal had placed on the ground. Jago looked at it; there were curious markings on the surface.

He couldn't understand them at all. There was a hole at the top—that must be for a string—and the thing at the bottom looked like the top of a thumb, small enough to belong to one of the elf folk. But what about the other signs?

Jago turned the stone over, but there was no help on the other side.

"The thing in the center is the sun, that's obvious," he said to himself. "But there *is* no sun down here, the elves can't stand it. Can it be a sundial? A kind of clock? No, they don't care about our sort of time. Oh, I wish they'd taken me with them."

He continued to study the stone, all the while thinking of the strange little people who had left it.

"Must have been something powerful in that drink they gave me last night. My legs feel strong enough to walk on. Legs! Walk! That's it. Why didn't I think of it before!"

Excitedly he grabbed the stone with both hands. Now that he

looked at it again, he could see that the markings under the sun thing were supposed to be legs: those on the left standing, those on the right walking. Yes, the legs on the right were definitely striding off somewhere. Jago saw that if they went on around the circle, they would pass all the other signs and eventually arrive at the pair of stationary legs—which was obviously where they were meant to stop. And there, right at that point, was a sign that could only mean one thing: a hole leading to water. The stone was a map of how to get to the sea.

Jago got up and began to examine the mine.

8

Taking the Plunge

Jago chose one of the passages at random and looked along it. Nothing there. He moved on to the next, seeking one of the signs on the stone. All the way around the mine shaft he went, examining the walls, the roof, the floor. He found nothing.

Then, just as he was about to give up, he saw, in a small dark shaft, the first of the signs. It was low down, a few inches from the ground, just where one of the small people would have carved it. His trail had started.

With some difficulty he set off along the low passage. It was cold and damp. Sharp stones cut his hands as he crawled along on all fours. He passed sign after sign, threading his way through the labyrinth.

The passages and tunnels twisted and turned; they widened into galleries and narrowed into small adits. Some parts were dry, but in others he had to crawl in a foot or more of icy water. He passed rooms full of rubbish, broken rocks, smashed tools, and all the clutter of a deserted mine.

The stone map was accurate; the signs appeared in the right order. The little people had not failed him.

Now he could hear the sea; a tiny speck of light in front of him grew and grew. Soon he could hear the cry of the sea birds, wheeling and darting beyond the cliff.

The last few yards of the passage were painful and slow. The drink that the elves had given him was losing its effect; his leg was beginning to throb with pain.

He pulled himself slowly to a window cut in the cliff, and looked out. The cliff dropped sharply beneath him, fifty feet or more, sheer to the sea. How was he to get out?

He craned his neck upward. There was a large rock overhang immediately above. No matter how near he might be to the cliff top, there was no getting out in that direction.

Directly below him was the sea. It was clear and sandy; he could almost see the bottom of it. A thought entered his mind. The sun was sinking now; if he was to do it, it had to be done soon.

Carefully, he edged out of the stone opening and maneuvered himself into a standing position, with his back to the sea. For a while he hugged the cliff, his heart pounding with fear. Then, gritting his teeth, he threw himself into the air, pushing away from the cliff with all his might.

His body arced. He hit the water with a crash and sank quickly.

The cold water was refreshing. Since Jago could swim like a fish, he was soon up at the surface and heading for the cove. Being in the sea was sheer delight after the cramped space of the tunnels, and the salt water soothed his sore body.

When he reached the shore, Jago lay for a while on the sand to dry off. The sun was dying into the red sea, its warmth fast vanishing. He got up as darkness fell and began hobbling inland, looking for a place to hide.

9

Spies

From the day that Jago fell down the mine shaft, a black cloud had been gathering in the minds of the people of Penwith. For from that date the Dark Lord began extending his influence even farther outside his estates, bringing fear and terror to the countryside. His anger at losing the Black Sigil of Pengersick was terrible. His men would suddenly descend on a house or farmstead, break in and search it thoroughly, smashing furniture and crockery in their wrath. People disappeared without explanation; barns and outlying bothies burst into flame late at night, with no clue to their destruction.

Mabby knew that in a way she could be held responsible for the pain and destruction, but she held fast to what the hermit had told her. She was more determined than ever to fight the sorcerer with any weapon that came to hand.

On the day that the Trenoweths' home was searched, a great disaster befell the Dark Lord. Men in leather jerkins, their fear of the zawn overcome by the blistering anger of their master, had roughly pushed their way into the cottage and begun turning the place upside down in the usual way. Suddenly, a dull, heavy, booming noise cascaded down the valley. It shook the whole cottage, making the shutters rattle and the jugs dance on the shelf. The sorcerer's henchmen rushed to the doorway and looked out. To the northwest, on the horizon, they saw a huge cloud rising from the high lands.

"Bal Dhu!" breathed one of the men. "Sun, moon, and stars, look at that!"

Even from where they were, they could see that part of the mountain had collapsed.

"Look lively, boys," shouted their leader. "I can't say what's happened for sure, but like as not we'll be needed up there."

With an excited yell the toughs vaulted onto their horses and thundered off.

Father Trenoweth looked hard at his family. " Bal Dhu. You realize what that means? Pengersick has set the little ones to mine for him. His lust for precious stones knows no bounds. The more they dig, the more he wants. But he's overreached himself this time, the mountain has become exhausted. And now it's caved in."

"Ah," said Mother Trenoweth. "And what about the poor people inside?"

"Still in the mountain," answered Father Trenoweth, shaking his head sorrowfully. "What cruelty, what shame for us after all the little folk have done for men!"

News of the disaster was swift to reach Pengersick. In his beautiful room at the top of the tower, the sorcerer swept the pieces off the gaming board with a trembling hand and threw himself back into his deep, carved chair.

"We managed to save these, my lord," said the messenger apologetically, passing him a bag full of precious stones.

The sorcerer poured them onto the table.

"Bah, more gewgaws, stones that any child can pick up on the beach. What of the black earth, have you got it yet?"

"My lord, this is all we have managed to extract besides the gems."

The messenger put a little wooden box on the table and opened the lid. The box contained a few spoonfuls of dark brown earth.

"You fool, this is common iron ore! I know the other is somewhere. That's how the place got its name—Bal Dhu, Black Mine. We must sink another shaft."

"My lord, all the adits have collapsed, the main shaft is full of rubble. We have recovered about ten guards and threescore miners. All the others are buried under hundreds of tons of rock."

"They'll survive," said the sorcerer heartlessly. "It's their element. Tell the officers in charge to get the mine open again by tomorrow!"

The messenger bowed low in fear.

"And take this dross to the steward, all of it!"

The man scooped up the pile of gems and hurried out.

The Master of Pengersick plunged into a cool pool of thought. Then he strode to the window and threw it wide open. He gave a high shrill whistle.

A moment later a ragged flapping of wings announced the arrival of half a dozen crows. They were bandy-legged, beady-eyed, ruffled, and dirty creatures, who hopped on the sill, pushing and bickering at each other.

"Hush, you miserable fowl," said the Dark Lord. "I want you to send out your forces to all the points of the compass. I want a spy at every crossroads, in every garden and farmyard, on every eave and sill of Pensans, Marghas Yow, Breage, and Hellys. Listen to every huckster and tinker; listen to every merchant and yokel; listen to the housewives chattering at the pump; listen to the fishermen mending their nets, to the children singing the latest news. And those of you that are owed favors by rats, weasels, and stoats, talk to them. Make them creep into barns, cowsheds, beerhouses, kitchens, and warehouses. Bring me news of the Black Sigil."

The sorcerer paused for a moment, letting his words sink in. The crows shuffled about nervously in front of him.

"To the one who brings me the news I hunger for, I will give a gift more precious than all others. I will give him a new human body to inhabit! Your former body if you want it, or a fresh one. You can choose any human creature in Penwith. His body will then be yours. Think of it, the gift of human life once more. Don't you all regret that you forced me to put you into those scrawny crows' carcasses? Here's your chance! Go and return with good news; and you will find me as generous as I can be cruel!"

With a cry of unsavory delight the crows took flight, caw-cawcawing the news to their underlings. Shrieking and chattering, the birds took off to the north, to the south, to the east, and to the west. Out they spread, furiously and intently winging their way in noisy competition for the great prize.

The sorcerer frowned and returned to his chair to brood over his misfortunes. A secret was eating at his heart, a secret he had never divulged to anyone. For every evil act he committed in the name of his secret, the pain grew worse. It made him daily more cruel; daily more wild and forgetful that he, too, was a man like other men.

10

Hanno

Jago had taken advantage of the disaster of Bal Dhu to make up lost ground. He had no particular end in view, apart from getting as far away from Pengersick as possible. He set off by hidden ways for the high moorland above the valley, where the gorse and heather thronged thick and the gray rocks were mottled with lichen. He would try and get a pony and ride off east, over Gwyntyreth, through Malpas, to Bosvenegh.

Limping along, he reached the edge of the moor and sat to rest on a low rock. After he had got his breath back, he realized that something was wrong; there was a tense silence over the land. No birds, that was it! No birds singing and twittering, no small furry creatures rustling the grasses; even the crickets were silent. He noticed a crow perched on a nearby thorn. The bird seemed to be looking at him inquisitively. No, it was just his imagination.

Jago opened his little bag and tipped out the contents: a scrap of pork fat, two sling stones, some flints and a steel, the stone he had been given in the mine, and the gold coin he had got from the sorcerer. As he looked at these things, he was sure that the crow had come nearer and was trying to see what it was he had.

What could an old black crow possibly want with him? Unless—and as he thought the thought his excitement mounted —unless the crow was a spy sent by the Dark Lord. Jago had heard that sorcerers were capable of making crows and small animals obey them. The crow could fly off at any second and give the alarm. He must stop it. He picked up a sling stone— but he had no sling!

Unknown to Jago, another pair of eyes was watching both him and the crow with great interest. A pair of eyes that looked down from far above the moorland. The possessor of those eyes had monitored Jago's progress through the fields and hedges, and had noticed that the crow was following him. The eyes belonged to a peregrine falcon, a slim and muscular bird of prey. Two years ago Jago had found it caught in a brier. He could have sold it to the falconers, but he nursed it back to health and fed it well. And then one joyful sunny day, he had taken it to the top of Castel an Dinas, and had let it go, watching it soar and wheel, higher and higher. He had named it Hanno. He had called out to it across the wind, and the bird, hesitating for only a moment, had returned and set a freshly killed rabbit at Jago's feet.

It was Hanno who now circled far above the ground, watching Jago. Hanno was worried about the crow, for much of the events of the last few days had reached him. He knew the crows were up to no good, and so he wheeled closer.

By now Jago was convinced that the crow really was spying. He threw a bit of pork fat invitingly onto the ground. The greedy crow, forgetting to be cautious, swooped on the morsel, and in that second Jago flung the stone. But he was tired by his recent exertions and the stone hit the bird too low to hurt. The black spy slithered and squawked, dropped the fat, and took off upward. Jago cursed as he saw the look of cruel treachery in the crow's bright eyes.

Then there was a rush, deadly, shrill, and swift, the heavy thud of talons hitting flesh, a gurgling shriek, and then a slow cloud of torn black feathers. Hanno turned, came beating back, and dropped the crow's broken body at Jago's feet.

Hanno landed nearby, calling out a greeting. Jago shouted joyfully at the bird and began piling stones on the crow's body. He did it thoroughly and, with a thin whistle that Hanno remembered well, set off again toward the moorland. Hanno flew above him, watching out for any more intruders, and in this way they soon arrived at the large rocks that lay, amid head-high brambles, just beyond the Trenoweth homestead.

Jago had been moving too fast for the good of his leg. As he reached the shelter of the rocks, a pain shot up his side; his breathing became difficult and he felt dizzy. He lay down in the shade and let the pain take him. With an eager rustle of wings the falcon landed nearby. He searched the area with his bright eyes before flapping over to Jago.

"Hanno!" said Jago. It was all he could think of to say. The boy and the bird looked at each other and understood each other's thoughts.

"Things are bad, Hanno. Even the wild creatures are divided against one another. That evil man has disrupted the harmony between man and beast, field and tree, sea and cloud. He sets crows to spy on men, men to destroy trees. Next he'll have the trees and herbs at war. Men have begun to act unjustly; fear does that. You've seen the ricks on fire, Hanno? Soon you'll see crowded gibbets, too."

There was a look of sadness in the bird's eyes, for all that Jago had said was true.

They both heard the sound at once. Hanno's neck twisted and his body arched for instant action. Jago slipped a long, thin knife from his belt and held it hidden by his side, his wrist tensed, ready to hurl the blade.

A small, worried voice called out from behind a nearby rock. "Don't move, Jago. It's me, Mabby!"

A thorn bush rustled and Mabby emerged, her frayed brown dress catching on the gray spikes. She wore her usual old clogs and held something tied up in her scarf.

"How did you get here? Oh, your leg!"

She knelt alongside Jago and looked at his injured leg. It was still slightly swollen, and around the wound his breeches were clogged with dried blood. She spoke quickly, excitedly.

"I saw it all happen, but I couldn't do anything fast enough. The Lord's men blocked the road and put a thorn fence around the top of the mine shaft. The others said there was no hope. But I knew, Jago. I just knew. The townspeople have even put up a stone to you near Polkimbro. It's exactly your height. It's got a pony carved on it and your name in edgewords. That's so the Dark Lord's men won't know what it says."

Jago grinned. Even if the Dark Lord's men found out that the stone was for him, it would only serve to allay their doubts as to his death.

"Mabby Trenoweth, do us a favor and get us some water."

"I'll do better than that, Jago Ponyboy. I'll take you where you can rest in safety and comfort. It's not far. Can you walk a bit?"

"With some help."

Mabby helped Jago to his feet and together they went deeper among the tumbled rocks, with Hanno flapping after them from outcrop to outcrop. The opening to the cave was difficult to approach, and impossible to find if one did not already know the way. It was screened by brambles as thick as sail rope, with thorns as large and sharp as arrowheads.

Mabby helped Jago carefully, showing him where to place his feet on the stony ground. At last they reached their destination. There was a small entrance area, a kind of hall, and then the main cave: a tall, cool place, with jagged cracks disappearing up into darkness. The floor was sandy. Mabby looked up at the roof.

"Can you see daylight up there? At night we can have a fire. The wind from the moors gets rid of the smoke. In the daytime we can use this."

She pointed to a small clay object that looked like a beehive.

Jago smiled. "Why, it's like a palace. A clome oven! It looks very old!"

"It's been here for years. People lived here a long, long time ago. I'm the only one who knows about it now. And you, of course. Have a rest. I brought up some water last night, it's the only thing we lack here."

Jago looked around the cave. It was the perfect hiding place. As long as it remained concealed, he would be safe. Since it had only one entrance, though, it was no place to fight from; there was no chance of escape. Better to fight in the open. He drank some of the cool water and drifted off into sleep.

When he awoke, it was night. A bright fire was crackling on the cave floor and a pot of vegetables bubbled over it. Mabby was feeding bits of meat to Hanno.

"Jago, what a clever bird. He killed a rabbit for your supper."

Jago sniffed. He could detect the savory smell of rabbit stew among the cooking vegetables. He sat up. His leg felt a little stiff, but apart from that it was fine. He managed to stand.

"How did you get out of the mine, Jago?"

"I was helped by the elves. What happened up at Bal Dhu?"

Mabby lowered her eyes.

"We all heard the mountain fall. Many of us went to try and help, but Pengersick had his men and dogs there. No one could get near. They say there was a rebellion. A lot of soldiers arrived, foreign soldiers paid for by Pengersick. It's said many of them went into the mine and did not return. The worst thing is that some of our people, who went over to the enchanter's side for the sake of gold, were ordered to fight the little folk. A lot refused, of course, and were punished. But it is known that some helped. There's much sadness in Penwith tonight. We can stand up to storms, hunger, and cruel lords. But can we hope to live a true life if we fight against our own consciences and souls?"

"It's all because of him," said Jago. "It's his way to turn people against each other. I have sworn to fight him."

Mabby looked up, her eyes shone with joy. "Jago, I have made a similar vow."

In a low voice she told him of the doe, of the hermit's potion, of her visit to Pengersick Castle. Jago listened open-mouthed to the exciting tale.

"But what can I do? I cannot leave my parents. All the spare time I have is now, at night, when I can slip out of the cottage and keep an eye on things. My parents depend on me."

"I have no parents, no responsibilities," said Jago. "I can devote all my time to fighting him. And Hanno will help. I'll go to Dunheved and see Kamren the archer, get him to make a bow for me. A war bow."

"Jago, the sorcerer does not rely on ordinary weapons. They are no use against him. If we wish to fight him, we will have to use things that can hurt him."

Jago's face darkened. "Do you mean . . ."

"Yes. I mean magic."

There was a cold silence in the cave. Then Jago said, "Magic can do evil things."

"Yes, Jago, of course it can. But look, magic is magic. It's not good, it's not evil. It's like a stream, it depends what you do with it. You can use a stream to flood villages, that's bad. Or you can use it to grow wheat, that's good. The stream is still just a stream."

"I don't know. Magic has a way of tricking the people who use it. You think you're doing good, you go on and on, and then you realize you're doing evil. I'd rather face him with a bow in my hand and a quiver full of good sharp arrows!"

"You'd never get near him. Even if you managed to get past his dogs and his guards and his walls, you'd find the arrows would melt in mid-air. We can defeat him only by getting some of his power and using it against him."

"I don't understand magic."

"I don't understand the wind or the sea, but I know what they can do."

Jago thought about it. He had begun to feel cramped in the cave, even though it was as big as a barn. He longed for the freedom of the open moors. He ate his stew steadily and carefully.

"Mabby, you're right. We can beat him only by using his own forces. But I'm just a simple pony boy from the moors. I can't read or write anything except edgewords. How am I to learn magic?"

"I can read. I can help you. Listen. I'll go to Pengersick Castle tonight. When I was there last I saw some of the Dark Lord's magic books. If I can get the right one, maybe we can find the root of his power. His magic must have had a beginning. If we follow his magic path it should lead us to the kind of power he's got. Then we can defeat him!"

She smiled with pleasure. The way she described it made it all sound so simple, and so exciting. Jago was just about to ask her if she wanted Hanno's help, when to his astonishment she uttered a strange word and began to fade like a mist. She became transparent, then disappeared.

A cold wind moved out of the cave, leaving it empty and silent.

11

The Fight at Gwynmaen

Jago finished the stew. It was the best he had tasted in a long time. Because he was alone in the world, he rarely bothered with cooking; he just ate what he could get.

He got up and began to explore the cave. It was bigger than he had thought. In places, the stone walls bore faint signs of the people who had lived there long ago. The piles of rocks around the base of the walls seemed to be spaced more regularly than was natural, but they had no purpose that Jago could discover. Behind the largest of them, so small and close to the ground that he almost passed it by, there was a hole. Curious, he reached his arm into the hole and then wiggled around until his head and shoulders were inside. In the total darkness he could see nothing, so he went back to the fire, lit the end of a branch to use as a torch, and pushed his way into the narrow opening. It was a short passageway. Jago could see that there was another room to the cave, a room so small that the flickering light from his branch showed him the opposite wall. He crawled into the room and stood up. Then he gasped with excitement.

In a corner was an old rotting box. He forced the lock and saw a jumble of things: a worn boot; a leather belt, green with mildew; some faded tunics; and, at the very bottom, something heavy wrapped in sacking. It smelt of faraway places and forgotten years. He undid the sacking and revealed an ax. Despite its being red with rust, Jago could see it was no ordinary woodsman's or carpenter's ax. It was something very special. It was half-size, but with a long, straight handle. It was made of engraved iron, and its head ended in a spike. He picked it up; it was beautifully balanced. When he swung it about, it made a swishing sound. Although he did not know it, the implement was a war-ax from a distant land, left there many years ago in haste.

Suddenly Hanno made a harsh noise. Jago dropped the branch and, carefully pushing the ax in front of him, crawled back into the main cave.

Hanno was alert, beak up in the air. He took off and flew out of the cave. Jago went to the entrance.

The stars had moved across the sky. He had not realized that time had gone so fast; it must be nearly two hours since Mabby had left. It had felt more like two minutes. Where was she?

No sooner had the question formed in his mind than he heard a rustling from the thorn brake, and the sound of hurrying feet.

Hanno came swooping down from the night sky, his cry of warning ringing through the rocks and making the hummocks of coarse grass shiver in fear.

Mabby materialized in front of him.

"Quick. Help me drag as much of that firewood inside as we can."

"What's the matter?"

"The Lord wasn't expecting me to go into the castle again, so I had no trouble getting a book, but he set wolves to patrol the grounds and, even though I was invisible, one of them saw the book as I crossed a clearing and a group of wolves is following. I have a good start on them, but they'll be here soon."

They pulled and tore at the pile of branches and logs that lay by the rock entrance. They dragged armfuls to the fire and thrust dry sticks into the embers. Mabby puffed at the glowing coals until they danced into life again. Then Jago had an idea.

"Over here, another fire. Bring those long branches. I'll get the wolves in this space."

"Here?" said Mabby. "You're going to let them come in here?"

Jago nodded and dragged blazing branches across the floor to start another fire.

"I thought we'd block the entrance, Jago."

"No, they must come in, all of them. If they escape, they'll tell the sorcerer. Hand me that ax."

Mabby hurried to get the ax.

"Where did it come from, Jago?"

"There's another room back there, behind that big pile of rocks. I found it in there just before you came."

Jago took a stone and dipped it into the jug of water.

"What are you doing?" she asked.

"Sharpening the ax. While I do this, you get lots of burning brands ready, and watch out for Hanno. He'll be flying about in here, so don't singe his tail feathers. If things get too bad, I want you to crawl into that other room and stay there."

Jago sat cross-legged on the ground and began carefully rubbing the stone across the rusted blade of the ax. He was as calm as if he were sitting on Kennack sands on a sunny day. He sharpened the edge of the blade until it gleamed. Then he put the stone down and tested the ax, making it whistle through the air.

From outside they heard a frightening sound: a snuffling sound, which started low and then began to get louder. Fiery red points of light danced about the cave entrance. Low, rippling shapes emerged from the darkness.

Jago grabbed a handful of burning branches from the fire and strode forward. With careless precision he tossed them at the slinking shapes. Cries of pain and rage showed he had not lost his skill.

The missiles that Jago had tossed at the first wolves lit up a wider area than that already brightened by the two fires. Jago stood ax in one hand, fire in the other.

There was a chilling howl from the darkness. It was the wolf leader ordering his raiders on to the attack. The animals answered his call and raced toward Jago. But they had to avoid the burning branches and the fires, so their phalanx was split up. Instead of surrounding him, they could reach him only in twos and threes.

Jago made no sound. He stood sideways with the fire held at arm's length in front of him, his ax loosely by his side. The beasts set up a ferocious clamor as they closed on him, fangs tearing and snapping, eyes bright red, mouths foaming.

The ax gave a note of impatience and came slicing down onto the head of the first wolf. It tumbled over, stone dead, its head split wide open. The blade came down again and again as the wolves leaped and charged; the fire stabbed at their eyes and ears, tails and mouths. The smell of burning fur filled the cave.

Mabby saw with terror that the wolves were working their way behind Jago. She picked up a blazing stick to hurl it, but before she could do so, another battle cry rang in her ears. Hanno swooped low with arched wings and razor-sharp claws. The wolf that had managed to sneak behind Jago had no time to turn its head. The falcon cut a furrow across its neck and muzzle, and turned to clutch at another wolf's eyes. As he rose up to the cave roof, Mabby threw her stick, and the two wolves were covered in a sheet of flame. They fled yelping out of the cave, and the others followed, tails low between their legs.

Jago flung his ember after them and stooped to pick up a fresh torch.

"They've had enough, Jago. We've won!"

"No, not yet. Keep back."

A deep howl announced the next attack. The wolves came into the cave again—all of them. They came angrily, leaping over the fires and the dead bodies of their fellows, eager to get

at Jago, eager to satisfy their hurt pride. They seemed to be everywhere at once, snapping, tearing, yowling.

Jago's ax never stopped. It had lost its dull rust color and was now bright and keen, shiny with blood. It began to whistle and hum, its battle cry blending with the shouts of the wolves and the shrill hunting call of Hanno.

And quite suddenly, after ten minutes of ceaseless cutting and slaughtering, it was nearly over. The floor of the cave was littered with bodies and only one beast was left to fight: the leader, a huge, grizzled animal with long, yellow fangs. It came forward slowly, eyes gleaming with hate, its strong back rippled with tense muscles.

The wolf leaped and Jago, stepping back to swing his ax, slipped in a pool of blood. The wolf cleared him completely and landed just in front of Mabby!

She was defenseless. Helplessly, Jago struggled to get up. The wolf leader bared his fangs in triumph and lunged at the girl. Then, with a shriek, he withdrew, for Hanno had landed on his head and thrust his talons deep into the animal's scalp.

As the wolf twisted in pain, Jago leaped across the cave floor and flicked his ax neatly down, severing the animal's skull from his body.

For a second everyone froze; time seemed to have stopped. Mabby stood in front of the wolf; Hanno perched on his head; and Jago stood behind it. The wolf gave a deep sigh and collapsed. He was dead.

Jago stared at the ax. It had changed. The rust had disappeared, and now they could see that the black iron of the blade was covered with intertwining animals and plants, all etched most skillfully with glowing gold inlay. There was writing, too: elegant curving lines of some outlandish script, mysterious and ancient.

They sat down and looked around them. The floor was littered with bodies and embers.

"Ugh!" said Mabby, pulling a face.

"It was like a dream," said Jago.

"Nightmare," said Mabby.

"There are no wolves left to tell where we are. This place is still safe."

"What shall we do with all these . . . bodies? We can't leave them here."

"I'll dig a pit in the thorn brake. I'll rest for a while and then do it before daybreak."

"I've got a better idea," said Mabby. "Not far from here is another cave. It's quite small, but we can put the bodies in there and pile rocks up in front. You'll never dig a pit without proper help."

Jago agreed, and they did as Mabby suggested, dragging the heavy gray forms into the cave, and blocking the entrance with rocks and branches. When they had finished, they returned to their hiding place and rested for a while by the fire. Mabby was the first to speak.

"I got the book, Jago. It's hard to read, the writing is so old and funny, but I think it's just what we need."

She produced the small volume bound in hairy gray skin. They opened it and gazed at page after page of curious diagrams and pictures.

"Here's a bit about magical apprenticeship. Oh, are you married, Jago?"

Jago kicked his heels in the air and hooted with laughter.

"Of course not. Why?"

"It says you must be free, pure, and without commitments such as a wife and family."

"What else?"

"Wait a minute. I'm trying to find out." Her eyes scanned the pages. "This is it. Listen. 'The operator'—that's you, Jago, it's got to be a man—must take a knife that's new and unused, and in the full moonlight cut with a single stroke a straight rod of hawthorn. This will be his wand. In order to store power in the wand, the operator must go on a journey alone, carrying with him no base metal of any kind, taking no money, and accepting no favor from any human being along the way. First to the Giants' Dance, Sol helps; thence to Carnac when the sky splits; and thence to Tara in the moon. Keep rod, take rod, then do as you may. Let the novice operator beware, lest the magic force spill and kill. This is the first method of obtaining power.' Well, it seems simple enough. Not like all those other complicated spells, that's all you have to do."

"Seems strange, not simple. Why do you look so sad, Mabby?"

"You will be gone for quite a while."

"I know."

"Oh, why can't I go? Just because I'm a girl . . . It's not fair."

"Mabby, watch what you say, don't let your hate for that man destroy us all. We've got to be very careful. There are important things for you to do. Keep a keen eye on Pengersick, and keep the ring safe. The Lord doesn't suspect you. You must keep the flame of hope alive in Penwith. We will win in the end."

"How are we to get a brand-new knife?"

Jago grinned. He took out the gold piece from his leather belt.

"Let's pay him back with his own coin!"

12

Blythcroghan

Next day Mabby went to market to buy a new knife for Jago. As the sun began to sink over Caer Bran, she returned to the cave.

"Here it is, Jago. Look how it shines!"

The boy held it up; it became red in the setting sun. It was the finest thing he had ever owned.

"There's all this, too," said Mabby, showing him a handful of silver. It was more money than she had ever handled before. She felt unsafe with so much in her possession. "Take it, Jago."

"We'll leave it here. You know I can't take it with me. If things get bad, you are to use it for whatever you think best. But for something good, mind!"

"Of course. Money's like magic."

"What were they saying in the market at Hellys?"

"A lot of gossip; people seem very scared. Some of those who made public complaints last week are now missing. Some have had their houses damaged. An old man got up in the market to speak, but everyone hissed at him and dragged him off. They are all afraid. The sorcerer's steward has been about a lot, talking to the layabouts, giving them money for drink."

The sun went down and a cold wind began to come in from the sea. From Pengersick, the wind carried the baying of hounds, taking the sound across the stones and turf of Trevurvas and Rinsey.

Jago shivered at the sound. He and Mabby went into the cave to read the spell book again. Jago repeated the requirements to himself until he knew them by heart. Then, when the moon rose full and silver, he went with Mabby to a hawthorn bush he had selected. All was quiet now, except for the voice of the breakers washing Trewavas Head two miles distant.

Jago took out the knife and grasped the thorn bush. He ignored the fact that the spikes tore at his hand, that blood spurted out and ran down his wrist. He steadied himself, his heart thumping louder than a storm off Porth Issick. A dreadful thought entered his mind: supposing he was unable to sever the thorn stick with one clean cut? If he failed to do that, then he was lost. He could not even begin his quest. He raised the knife and brought it down as hard as he could onto the growing bush.

Something was wrong, something was dragging at his arm. The knife moved painfully slowly through the air, as if trying to escape from a powerful magnet, a magnet that was holding it back from hitting its target.

Jago sweated and grunted, pushing the knife toward the bush. It seemed to be stuck in mid-air. He exerted more effort, and the knife blade, white in the moonlight, at last reached the wood and slowly began to cut into it. With a gasp of triumph, Jago relaxed.

The knife hung limply at his side, as if the metal itself were exhausted. In his other hand, Jago grasped the thorn stick— which he had cut off with a single blow!

Silently, he trimmed the stick of its prickles and shoots. He looked at the blade and felt the back of it with his hand.

"Ouch! Feel, the knife's hot."

"Who would have thought it," said Mabby wonderingly. "What do we do with it now?"

"Bury it," answered Jago.

He knelt and pushed the knife into the earth. It hissed as it went through the grass and there was a slight smell of burning. Jago took a stone and tapped the end of the knife handle with it, until all trace had disappeared into the ground. Then he stood up happily and lifted the thorn stick in the moonlight.

"We did it, Mabby. Cut it through with one clean cut."

"It went so fast I hardly saw it!"

Jago stopped and looked at her. "Fast? You mean that?"

"Of course, that knife went through the air faster than a snake's tongue."

Jago frowned. "I see . . ."

"Let me hold it," said Mabby.

"Yes, in a minute. Let's get back."

The moon was still silver and bright as they returned to the cave. Mabby studied the thorn stick, while Jago got together the things he would need for his journey.

"It's just an ordinary stick," she said. "I don't see anything magical about it."

"We have to be patient, you know what the spell book says: Know, Will, Dare, Keep Silent. That goes for both of us. There, I'm nearly ready."

He wore his old jerkin and breeches, and had wound cloths around the lower part of his legs. On his feet he had a pair of leather moccasins as protection against thorns and sharp gravel. In the small bag at his belt he had salt, grain, a lump of cheese, a flint knife, and some tinder for firemaking.

"I wonder why you're not allowed any metal," said Mabby. "Making fire with sticks is much more trouble."

"Oh, I won't have much time for all that, anyway. Look, I've got something to show you."

Out of a dark corner he picked up a bundle and undid it. Teeth gleamed, and for a moment Mabby thought a gray wolf was springing at her out of the gloom.

Jago laughed. It was the skin and head of the wolf king. He

had made it into a cloak. He placed it around his shoulders; the dead wolf's head, with its long fangs, rested on top of his own.

"A new cloak to start my journey with."

"You look fierce enough to scare off any strangers you might meet."

"Yes, and if anyone asks me my name I have one to tell them. Jago Blythcroghan!"

"Jago Wolfskin. It sounds better in the old Kernewek."

"Everything does. I spoke no other tongue until I was ten years old. No one speaks it now."

"We will speak it when you return."

They stood in silence; then Jago said, "I must go. I reckon to keep up a good smart pace to the Tamar, after that I'll have the moors to deal with."

Outside the cave, he gave a high whistle, and from a nearby brake came the sound of a pony's answer—a low, rough whinny.

Mabby leaned forward and kissed Jago on the cheek. Then she turned and ran back toward her parents' cottage. Jago walked to the pony that had been patiently waiting, and vaulted onto his back. He clicked his tongue, and the animal, sensing the urgency, set off at a good smart pace, just as Jago had said. By daybreak, if all went well, they should reach the ford at Malpas.

Jago whispered encouragement in the pony's ear and set his head to the northeast.

13

Pengersick's Secret

That night in the tower of Pengersick, all seemed quiet. The dogs in their kennels, the horses in their stables, the guards in the barracks, all slept soundly. Up at his window the Lord of Pengersick was awake and listening. All he could hear was the sigh of the surf as it stroked the sands of Prah and, from time to time, the stump and clank of the watchman as he went his rounds.

The sorcerer loved these hours of darkness. He felt free from the petty troubles that filled the daylight hours, glad that he did not have to deal with foolish humans. His concerns could never be their concerns; for in truth, he did not care if he drank water or wine, ate dry bread or exotic foods, wore homespun clothes or fine befurred silks. He had known all states of comfort and discomfort, all moods of pleasure and pain, and now he did not care about such things; they were as unimportant to him as a fly on the windowpane. It is true he lived in some style, but men were impressed by such outward show. They would fear him less if he displayed poverty. His wealth did not influence his mind from its set purpose.

It was now, in these dark hours, that the sorcerer gave in to his most secret thoughts.

He rose from his chair and took a bunch of keys from a box. He left his rooms and trod softly down the unlit stairs. He passed two guards asleep at their posts, and paused to remove their knives and tie them up with their own ropes. He would punish them later.

He went down into the dungeons, where the smell of the sea mixed with the odor of decay and damp earth. In one corner was a well. The sorcerer went across to it and, setting himself carefully in the bucket, let slip the noiseless rope until he sank into the shaft. Down and down he lowered himself, until the bucket arrived at a small passageway leading off the main shaft. He got out and walked along it, to a room that echoed to the boom of the sea. The room shined with translucent light.

He approached a filigree casket of gold, set on a plinth, that was the source of the light. Peering into the brightness, he could see the low, squat shape of the creature whose being was trapped inside the casket.

The sorcerer walked past the imprisoned toad to a long wooden box, covered in a rich cloth. Slowly he pulled the material away. The action disturbed rich incense, which rose to assail his nostrils. He gazed at the box.

For the next three hours he remained there, standing as still as a post, gazing with wide, dark eyes; gazing so hard one would have thought he could see straight through the close-grained teak.

At the end of that time his senses twitched; he thought he had caught a scent that was familiar, but out of place here. A warm, salty scent, reminiscent of the sea, and of sea voyages and the memory of sea voyages. But it was soon gone under the waves of exotic perfume that emanated from the wood of the long box. He looked around.

He saw nothing.

14

Across the River

Jago went as fast as the ponies would take him. He did not follow the normal tracks, but allowed the animals to use their own secret ways. When one pony lessened its speed, there would be another waiting to take over, and then another. A relay of animals waited silently across the moors. He did not question their presence. It seemed that all had been alerted by that sense of collectiveness that humans lack.

All day he rode, with faithful Hanno circling above him. At midday he stopped to drink at a stream, and Hanno settled nearby to eat a plump shrew he had killed.

Jago had traveled on the ponies before. He knew that they would take him as far as the other side of Bosvenegh moor; but they would not cross the river. Like Jago, they were unacquainted with the land over the river, and distrustful of it. As far as they were concerned, it was a foreign country. By using the ponies he was keeping within the terms of the spell; if he was to survive, he must be careful on the other side not to accept any help from humans.

At last they reached the bleak and open spaces of the high moors; over, past Bosvenegh town, he went, in rain that fell from a leaden sky. No one saw him go. He saw the tumbling rain clouds mirror the billowing moors and challenge their blackness. He passed by Pol Doz, that inland sheet of water shunned by honest folk who feared the ghostly sails that were sometimes seen there, and went down into the thick forests that bordered Kilmartor, Caradon, and Kit.

On the morning of the next sunny day, he let his last pony go, and walked the final few miles down to the river. Hanno landed nearby and called out to him cheerfully. Jago emptied his little bag of the last of the food.

"The end of my country, the end of my food. I'll make a fire and crack the grain."

As he went to work, Hanno flew off. He returned just as Jago had heated a flat stone on which to parch the grain; his shadow fell across the fire.

"Hey, bucca boy, what's this? A rabbit for our farewell meal!"

Jago took out his flint knife and skinned and gutted the small animal.

"How shall we have it? If I roast it all, there'll be enough food here for three days."

He threaded the meat onto thin sticks and set them so that it would roast. Then he looked at the river. There was no ignoring the fact: the river was there and had to be crossed. He had reached the end of his world; he had reached the end of the land of Kernow. The river seemed wide and deep; there was nowhere to cross. He wondered . . .

"Garralooks! Meggameggameeeeee!"

Jago yelped in terror at the fearsome cry. He grabbed his flint knife and held it out defensively as a strange creature leaped, gibbering, from out of a nearby tree. The thing stopped and looked at Jago and his knife, and then burst out laughing. It laughed and laughed until it rolled on the ground.

"Oooh . . . hooo, your face. Oh my, oh my, your face, hoo . . . hoo . . . hoo!"

Jago's face turned to anger.

"Who are you, you jackanapes, you greasy slubgullion?"

"Jackanapes! Oooh . . . hooo . . . oooh . . . hooo . . . oooh . . . hoo!"

"I beg you to hold your tongue, sir, and explain yourself." The thing looked surprised. Jago added, "Instantly!"

The thing sniffed. "Instantly is very soon," it said, preening its multicolored clothes. It had a bony face and a tall cap.

"Instantly is now!" retorted Jago.

"Ah, I see. Well, how am I to explain myself? I was born many years ago in a small village not far from—"

"I don't want your life story. In fact, I dislike your whole attitude. Good day to you."

"Oh, come, young master wolfslayer, have pity. I only meant to entertain you. I need your help, you see. I have to cross this river and meet my company. Else they'll kick me out for sure. I missed them at Dunheved Fair and wandered down the river too far, drank too much mead, and went to sleep."

The person—Jago could see it was human and not some monster—stood near the fire, sniffing the delicious smell of cooking rabbit.

"Food! I'm starving. I've not eaten a thing since yesterday morning. Do you think, young lad, I might have just . . ."

"Help yourself, you should have said you were hungry . . ."

But the man had grabbed a hunk of tender rabbit and had already sunk his teeth into it. Jago watched in amazement as he gobbled at the meat.

"Ummm, delicious, are you not eating?" the man said, his mouth full.

"If I eat now, I won't eat on the moors."

"What? You are planning to go alone across the Greymoor, with only a day's food?"

"I was. And that was three days' food the way I eat it."

The man looked ashamed; he stopped eating.

"It's impossible for anyone to go over the moor alone, even

with a wagon of food. It's terribly dangerous, believe me. That's why I must reach my company. We're going over with some archers and merchants. It's the only way nowadays. Here!"

The man clicked his fingers and produced an egg, as if out of the air. He cracked it open on his bony knee.

"Oh dear, it's hard-boiled. I only eat soft-boiled. Here, you have it, wolfslayer. In trade for the rabbit."

He tossed the boiled egg toward Jago, who caught it, but then hesitated.

"Go on, it's fresh."

"Why were you hungry if you can catch eggs out of the air like that?"

"It's part of my act . . . I'm a jester, you see. I'm really fed up with eggs, especially when I smell rabbit!"

Jago smiled and bit into the egg; it was tasty.

The man in motley went on. "It's true what I just said. It's dangerous to travel on the moors; you must come with us. Of course, you'll have to work if you can't pay, but we badly need helpers. You'll get fed as well. Or you might do better driving a line of pack horses—the merchants are always crying out for help. You see, it's difficult to get people to go across the moor. Three days it takes, and no one's safety is guaranteed. You can't make it alone, boy, even if you can kill wolves. Wolves are chickens compared to what's up there."

Jago took a bit of rabbit and said, "Well, if there's food to be earned we might as well finish this up."

With that he tossed the meat high into the air. The jester gasped as Hanno swooped low and grabbed it.

"What a trick! A trained falcon. Hey, do that again!"

"No. The bird's a friend, not a performing clown."

"Ah." The man's face darkened.

"I'm sorry, I didn't mean to offend you."

"I understand. Well, what's your name?"

"Jago Blythcroghan."

"Well, Jago, are you coming with us?"

"Yes, but first let's get over the river."

Jago stamped out the fire and scattered the embers. Then he pointed with his thorn stick at the river, and Hanno rose in the air.

"What now?" asked the man.

"We wait."

They shielded their eyes as Hanno flew in a wide circle; he returned and headed off in the other direction. They saw him hover, his wings beating the air steadily, his slim body poised like a signpost.

"That's it, he's spotted somewhere we can cross."

"Hooray, what a splendid fellow," shouted the jester, as they rushed to the place where Hanno was keeping station.

"Stepping stones!" He began leaping across them happily. "Come on."

Jago set his feet on the first stone and looked across the river. A sudden doubt had entered his mind. Was he doing the right thing? Why had he got mixed up in this madness, anyway? Why was he here so far from home? Then he remembered the sorcerer and gripped his thorn stick tightly. Yes, he must go on. He began to go from stone to stone, but found it difficult. The distances between them seemed to be getting wider and wider; the stones were slippery with moss and water. The sound of the river increased to a roar as if the wolves had at last got him.

"Come on, lad, come on," called the jester.

Jago looked backwards. It seemed to him that there were figures there on the bank he had just left: figures whose vague outlines were veiled by a light mist; faint gray shapes, waving, shouting, running up and down. He thought one of them was Mabby. Were they calling him back? Was there treachery ahead? Who was that jester anyway?

Jago called out, "I must go back, they need me. I should never have left them."

"No, Jago, come on, there's nothing there," shouted the jester. "Your mind is playing tricks on you. Come on."

"Mabby, is that you? Answer me!"

"They can't speak. Whatever it is you are seeing does not exist. You must keep moving, Jago!"

Jago managed three more stones; he was exhausted and wet through. Fear raged through his mind; fear and doubt. He said a prayer to the land he was leaving behind him.

"Farewell, Kernow. I must go to another place whose earth I have never walked, whose air I have never breathed, whose water I have never drunk, and whose food I have never tasted. Remember me and I will return."

With tears blurring his eyes, Jago ran quickly across the remaining stones and collapsed on the bank.

"Jago Blythcroghan, what was all that about?"

"Have they gone?" asked Jago weakly.

"I cannot say, I saw nothing. Only you can tell."

Jago raised his eyes and looked back across the river. The far bank was empty, not a soul in sight.

After they had rested awhile, the jester got to his feet.

"Come on," he said, "it's time we made a move. We must get to that town before they leave to cross the moor."

He pointed ahead to where low roofs clustered about a stone tower.

He shaded his eyes.

"Oh no. They've started, we'll have to run, boy."

Jago saw a line of horses, smaller than mice at this distance, slowly climbing the road that led from the town to the moor. He set off after the jester, and they ran the last mile in silence.

15

Greymoor and the Wishing Stone

The line of horses seemed endless to Jago. In fact, there were about fifty of them, all burdened with great panniers or pulling small carts that swayed on the narrow track. As they trotted past the rear guard, Jago and the jester were greeted by a variety of strangers. Then, from a brightly painted cart ahead of them, came a low, gruff noise.

"Who's in pain?" asked Jago. "Sounds serious."

"Oh, don't you worry about that," said the jester, suddenly looking embarrassed.

The noise grew louder as they approached the cart; a weird assortment of people were riding in it and clinging to the sides.

"These must be the strolling players," thought Jago. "The company, as my jester friend calls them. What a strange lot!"

All the people were groaning as if in agony, and they pointedly ignored the jester, even though they must have seen him approach.

"They are just having a little fun at my expense," said the jester, and he yelled out, "Well, I must say it's been a refreshing change to be with good company. I have persuaded a valiant hero to accompany us across the moor. His name is Jago, and he kills wolves!"

"Hail, Jago."

"Know any good stories, Jago?"

"Where are you bound, Jago?"

70

"Where do ye come from . . ."

"What an odd name . . ."

"Jago? Sounds foreign. Oh, he's a Map Kernow. Yes, he is foreign!"

A burly man rode up. He was dressed in a thick leather jerkin and carried a short white stick to show he was in command. His face was stern but wise.

"I'm Armel. Welcome, lad, we need active men. You can get a job with one of these fat-bellied merchants—or you can come with me, stand guard, and be prepared to fight for the common good. You'll get the same foul food as we eat and a brass penny when we reach Sarum Goose Fair. To tell you the truth, any of these merchants will give you more for just holding their horses. Well, what's it to be?"

Jago looked at the merchants, who were eyeing him speculatively. He knew that if you worked for one of them you were responsible for him and his horses alone. If disaster befell the community, then too bad for the rest: the merchants would look after their own goods and safety and let the others go hang.

"I'll come with you, sir," he said to Armel.

"Good."

"Wait awhile, good sirs. Jago here is my guest."

"Thank you, Jester," said Jago. "I appreciate that, but I must earn my keep like all the rest. I'll not be beholden to anyone."

Armel smiled. "Well said, the jester can help us too!"

"Not me," said the jester.

"A jester and a boy make up half a man," shouted one of the soldiers.

"And they both together will get half a man's food," called another jokingly.

"I'll make you half a man if you don't hold your tongue," said the jester, and turned a cartwheel, kicking mud into the soldier's face.

"No bickering in the company," shouted Armel. "The Greymoor lies ahead—we must be united."

With that he rode off down the trail. It was not a job he liked, shepherding a group of merchants, tradesmen, and artisans over the moor.

"What danger can there be?" Jago asked the jester.

"My lad, last week a whole group of travelers disappeared. Then a group of sailors, crossing the Greymoor to find work on the coast, were also attacked. Some of them staggered back alive, but their wits had gone. They are crazed men; their sanity was destroyed by what they saw."

"Is there a safer way around?"

"You tell me. You can always take a ship and risk getting fatally wet on the jagged coast. At least this way we've good land beneath our feet. Why, there are even some sailors among the guards—it must be safer than the sea."

"What manner of evil is it?"

"Some enchantment, they do say."

The hairs on Jago's neck stood stiff at the words, his face drained with fear. Who else but Pengersick had such power?

"Don't worry, lad, we'll soon be over the moor and heigh-ho for Sarum Fair. There'll be music and dancing there. Have you ever tasted roast Sarum goose with chestnut and apple stuffing? Ah, there's a kingly dish, and cider, too, from the vale. Such a time we'll have, Jago, with money to clink in our pockets, and new hats with feathers as tall as Armel's great bow!"

"Isn't the Goose Fair to celebrate some pagan worship of the sun, or something?"

"Ohhh, yes, I believe there's some sort of funny old ceremony up at the Giants' Dance. Some people get upset by it, but I prefer to leave such things alone . . . What a good time we'll have, the maidens with nut-brown legs and cheeks like ripe apples, dancing bears, and of course my company of lads and lassies. But mind, keep close to us this journey, lad. There's danger ahead. I can smell it."

Jago shivered as the jester spoke, for the sun had gone and a great shelf of yellow-gray cloud had wedged itself into the sky. The beginnings of a fog had begun to creep up from the marshes and the small bog-filled valleys. The laughter from the players' carts was less frequent; people began to bunch together and draw their cloaks closer about their shoulders.

Soon the talking stopped altogether. The travelers seemed to be listening for something other than the steady clump-clump of the horses' hoofs and the tinkling of the bells on the merchants' reins.

"Keep close, Jago, you never know what's out there."

But Jago was unconcerned. He walked along, keeping pace with the slow horses, casting a glance from time to time at the sky to see if Hanno was about. He could easily miss the pack-train in this fog.

A throaty growl made Jago look around. A small dog stood up in one of the carts, staring into the swirling fog, its ears up, its hackles tense.

"Summat out there, I'll be bound," said one of the soldiers. Jago saw him check his bow.

But nothing happened. Darkness fell at last, and Armel called a halt. He pointed to a flat, dry, grassy plot, and with much shouting and cracking of whips the carters made a defensive circle of their vehicles. The pack animals were tethered inside it. Fires were lit, and smoke, as thick as the fog itself because of the wet peat, began to billow.

"Why are we stopping here?" complained a plump merchant. "Nether Farm was to be the first stop."

"Then find it yourself in this fog," retorted a soldier.

"Where are we?"

"No one knows, not even Armel!"

"Someone said we've come a different route to avoid trouble."

"If you ask my opinion we're good and lost."

And so they grumbled and chatted as they began to prepare their meal. Although it was now night, the fog was still so thick that not a star could be seen.

"No stars, eh?" said the jester. "It's a bad night without stars, Jago. Can't tell where we're headed."

"Oh, it'll all clear up."

"Well, you seem to be very relaxed."

"I've spent worse nights than this on the moors; so must you have. Why's everyone making such a fuss?"

"It's the merchants. They've got such a lot to lose, it makes them act like fussy hens."

Suddenly, a wild despairing cry rang out through the camp. Alarmed men leaped to their feet, swords glinting; others ran to quiet the horses, who snorted and bucked at the sound. Some men stood stiff with fear, unable to move.

"Quieten those beasts down, lads. Everyone keep a watch out. No, don't move, curse you! Now, look about you, at your friends, anyone missing?"

People began calling across the space.

"Hey, Will?"

"Dickon, you safe?"

Armel asked again. "Anyone missing?"

"Only the dog! The players' dog."

The players started calling and whistling for their dog. There was no reply.

"Don't care for this much." The jester shivered.

"Let's go and take a look," said Jago impatiently.

"No one moves without permission from Armel," said a soldier.

Jago ignored him and began strolling off.

"Armel, the boy's trying to go."

Armel's voice sternly thundered across the night. "Stay where you are, boy. No one leaves the ring until daybreak. I'm responsible and I say no one is to leave."

"No one is responsible for me, except me," replied Jago.

Armel looked at him angrily. "Get back to the fire."

"That boy is bad luck," said the plump merchant. "Never had any trouble before he joined us. Who is he anyway, and why's he wearing that moth-eaten wolfskin? Wants us to believe he killed a wolf, eh, that the big idea? The dirty-nosed gypsy brat."

"Hold your prating tongue, sir! He's got the look of a brave man, which is more than I can say for you. He has the look of destiny about him," said Armel.

"Destiny?" sneered the merchant. "His destiny is to try and lead us astray, lead us into an ambush."

"If you don't hold your tongue," said Armel, "you and your beasts can leave. Well?"

The man fell silent.

"All right, everyone get some sleep. We start early tomorrow."

Jago wrapped his cloak about him and lay down by the fire. He heard the merchant whispering and complaining, telling anyone who would listen that the boy was bad luck and ought to be abandoned. The merchant had a valuable load and he wasn't going to be cheated of it by some scruffy peasant. Had it been a normal time Jago would have punched the man's fat nose; but now he was a candidate for magic, he felt he had to learn to ignore such trivial things.

Later that night, when the travelers were all fast asleep, Armel selected two of his men and slipped quietly out of the camp. They scouted in a wide arc and discovered the trail again. They were on their way back to camp when one of the men stopped suddenly and pointed.

"Look over there."

Spears and bows at the ready, they approached a huddled form lying on the ground. It was the missing dog, or what was left of it. It had been torn apart.

"Say no word of this to anyone," ordered Armel. "By stone and star, that wolfskin would have run into trouble if I had let him venture out!"

The two men kept their peace. Even the next day, when they saw the players calling and whistling for their dog, they did not tell what they had seen. The fog had cleared now and the moor lay before them, its gray, humped shape looking like a frozen sea.

The jester picked up a bone and spent the morning whittling away at it with his knife.

"What are you doing?" asked Jago.

"I'm making a pipe of this bone. The wind that roams these moors has blown it clean and knows it well. If the fog comes and brings trouble, and we need to see our way clearly, I can call up the wind with this."

"Is it magic?"

"No more magic than the wind itself. Don't you believe it will work?"

Jago shrugged. "Will it help us if we were attacked by those men out there?"

"What men? Where?" The jester's mouth fell open in fear.

Jago pointed. On the ridge, not too far distant, were half a dozen hunched shapes, traveling in the same direction as the pack-train. The jester's face went white.

"Armel knows already. I saw him looking at them an hour ago. I would not have spotted them else."

"If Armel knows, then we are safe," said the jester. "Look, we have come to the wishing stone."

The line of horses had stopped in a kind of valley. The nearby ridge was crowned with a strange rock formation: a large stone, balanced by itself at the highest point. Travelers were leaving their horses and carts and eagerly scrambling up the slope.

"It's the wishing rock," said Jago's friend. "Not heard of it? No one ever goes across the moor without coming here. You go up to it and tell it your wish. If the rock moves, your wish will be granted. If it doesn't move . . . well, come and try again in a year's time."

"Have you been here before? Did your wish come true?"

"Not allowed to say!"

They took their place in the line. Jago noticed Armel had posted guards. He watched the rock; it didn't appear to move for anyone. The fat merchant went up and whispered as strongly as he could; he even tried to move the rock with his hand, but it didn't budge an inch. The merchant came away, looking annoyed.

"Childish superstition! What a waste of time. Why don't we get moving?" he said bitterly.

The jester went up and delivered his wish. The rock remained firm. He climbed down quietly, smiled, and said, "Your turn, Jago, hope you have better luck."

Jago went to the rock. He was the last one. Most of the other travelers had already regained their horses, or were scrambling down the slope. He whispered and waited.

And waited. Then the unbelievable happened. The rock began to sway and roll; it shook and made a deep rumble that echoed down the valley. Jago sprang back in fear; it seemed as if the rock would topple over. The travelers and guards looked up in amazement.

"What is it?" someone called.

"Young wolfskin's got his wish!"

"What did you ask for, Jago?"

"A pot of gold?"

"A fair wench?"

"I know—a flock of sheep!"

The fat merchant sneered. "His good fortune is likely to be our bad fortune. He cheated. He moved it himself."

But no one listened to him. They smiled at Jago, and some touched his wolfskin cloak with their fingers or talismans to try and get some of his luck.

"I hope you asked for a safe journey, lad," said Armel.

Jago looked at him, then he looked at the horizon and saw that the party of men had grown to at least a dozen.

There was a shout from ahead. They saw that the band of wild, shambling men was not the only one; there was another group blocking the route in front of them.

"All right now, don't panic. Keep your swords loose in your scabbards. And string your bows."

16

Jago Draws Blood

Jago counted about twenty wild men in the front rank alone. They made a deafening din as they beat short wooden cudgels against round leather shields.

"Looks as if they mean business," said the jester. "Hey, boy, take this!"

He offered Jago a knife with a steel blade.

"No, thank you," said Jago, and took out his flint knife.

"What's the use of that?"

"It doesn't get rusty," Jago replied. There was another great yell from the moor men, and one, who appeared to be their leader, shouted a string of uncouth words in their dialect. A soldier with moor men's blood in his veins translated.

"They want the wolfskin boy. If we give him to them, they will let us pass in peace. They want to sacrifice him to their Beast God."

"What did I tell you," shrieked the fat merchant. "What did I tell you. Now give them the brat before they smash our skulls in."

"Donner, take your bow and three men to the knoll. We'll need cross fire. Steady, everyone else."

"I can see at least fifty of them, Armel. And remember, they always keep most of their men out of sight until the battle starts. It's the only trick they know. I'd say they've got another eighty or ninety hidden nearby."

"Every man we see represents a family," said the interpreter. "He'll have at least a father, son, or brother somewhere behind him."

"Give them the boy," muttered another merchant.

"Yes, give 'em the boy."

Jago leaped forward and turned to face the travelers.

"No one gives me to anyone. I'm my own responsibility, I don't belong to any of you. I'm not a slave, I go and come as I choose. Let me through!"

He revealed himself to the wild men, who set up another shout.

"No!" said Armel. "I'm in charge here. Soldiers, grab hold of the lad, get ready your arrows."

But before the soldiers could move, Jago had slipped through. They watched in horror as he calmly advanced on the moor men, who chanted and yelled. Jago lifted his thorn stick and gave a whistle. With a fierce cry, Hanno came swooping down and landed on the point of the stick; he balanced there, wings apart.

A gasp of astonishment broke from the moor men. Jago, with his gray wolfskin cloak blowing in the wind, the savage head of the wolf resting on his tousled hair, and his raised stick with the bird on top of it, was an emblem of half-remembered fear. Down in their dim folk memory they recalled a similar figure, and the recollection of it struck mortal terror into their hearts. The moor men huddled together; all at once they had lost their savage power. They were merely a group of vacant-eyed animals, dressed in the cast-off clothing of shepherds and what few garments they had taken from the bodies of travelers they had slain.

The leader shook himself and grunted. Now was the time to assert his predominance, to show his men what he was made of. He came forward, menacingly.

Jago fixed his eyes steadily on the man as he advanced. The wild man roared and swung his club; Hanno flew off, and Jago side-stepped. The man hit out again. Jago pulled out his flint knife in a wide arc, and, as the man came forward for the third time, he slashed him across the forehead with it.

The leader howled, staggered, blood pouring from his open wound. Jago smashed his stick across the back of the man's knees and he fell like a stone; groaning with pain, he scrambled back to his lines.

Another, younger moor man emerged. He rushed at Jago. Instead of side-stepping as the man had expected, Jago ran at him. Again the flint knife swept through the air and tore a furrow across the man's brow.

At this, the whole pack yelped and fled. Their two strongest fighters had been beaten. The wolfboy must have stronger magic than their Beast God. They would have to find their blood sacrifice elsewhere.

When they saw the moor men retreating, the travelers cheered. The soldiers looked at each other, eyes bright with approval at what they had witnessed. Armel shook his head with wonder.

"Masterly, masterly. The boy's a natural warrior."

The jester shared fully in Jago's triumph; he turned somersaults for joy and stuck his tongue out at the fat merchant.

Above, Hanno dipped and wheeled. Then he turned and flew back the way they had come. The bird had watched over the boy since their journey had begun; now it was time to return to his native haunts, to the land and sky that was his home. It was to be many months before Jago would see him again.

"Let's get moving," ordered Armel.

"We've not seen the last of that lot," declared the fat merchant.

"Shut your mouth, pig-belly," yelled the jester. "Saved your fat paunch, didn't he? He's just a boy, but he's more of a man than you!"

"Come on, we must make up for lost time," said Armel, but there was a smile on his lips.

"I smell fog," said one of the sailors. "Let's make as much headway as we can."

17

Fogwalkers

The horses and men set off at a good pace. Encouraged by the new freedom from worry, nearly all had smiles on their faces. They all chattered excitedly about the skirmish.

Armel took them along a trail that led as straight as a shaft of sunlight to the horizon. The road, a sign of man's presence in the moorland wilderness, made everyone feel good. It was as if an invigorating force flowed along the road, protecting and renewing all who walked or rode on it.

"I've never seen a trail as marvelously straight as this one. Who made it?" asked Jago.

"We make it every time we travel along it," said a kind-looking merchant with gray hair. "Look," and he pointed.

Jago looked down the road and saw that it headed directly toward a cairn, which stuck up from the distant horizon.

"A sight mark," said the merchant. "You just go from one to the other—cairns, ponds, stones, fords, bridges, mounds. All have been set to guide the traveler across the land."

The jester joined in the conversation. "Over there the road leads to Treglas, where in a crystal hall under the hill sleeps an olden king. His warriors lie with him, dressed in golden mail, helms on their heads, axes and swords clutched in their cold hands. And around the hill itself sleeps a coiled dragon."

"Aye? Is that all true?" asked Jago suspiciously.

"So they do say. Not seen it myself, mind you. But it's also said that when this realm is in sorry state, when the dark clouds threaten and the storm wrack hurls on the beaches, then a man without blame or shame will raise a silver hunting horn to his lips, and by blowing three long blasts will raise the sleepers from their deep doom."

"What then?"

"Ach, lad. Terrible battles, I'll be bound."

Jago shivered.

"That day's long to come, lad. It'll be when men have forgotten to talk to animals, stones, and trees. When they no longer live as part of nature but opposed to it."

"But nature will ever be with us. Man has to breathe air, drink water," said the merchant.

"I don't know," said the jester. "I just repeat the old stories. It's not for me to question them, that would be like the flute commanding the flute player. No, I'm just the flute on which the old stories play whatever tune they want."

"Aye, true, true," said a strange voice. The three of them looked around at the man who had just joined them. He was a square-built, hard man. He wore black gloves and had a gold ring in his ear.

"Pardon, sirs, but you spoke of things near my heart. I am Madoc ap Arthus, son of Arthus ap Olwen, from the land of Gwent. I am bound for the place where the sun rises, for I have taken a vow to travel as far as man can go in that direction. I have a great desire to reach the world's edge and look over it into the gulf beyond. I go because I, too, am a flute being played upon by fate. Everyone at home says I'm mad."

He laughed uneasily, for as he had been speaking the fog had come down again. The horse bells tinkled eerily through the gloom, and the plodding animals sent clouds of steam up as the cold mist met their hot flanks.

There was a cry of alarm as one of the advance guard, sent ahead by Armel, came spurring back to report.

"Something moving out there, on both sides of the track. Huge shapes, moving slowly, difficult to catch a glimpse of what they are."

"Keep your stations, see that no one strays," ordered Armel.

"Is it the moor men again?"

"Who knows?"

"Too big. I saw one as tall as a young tree!"

"Halt! Everyone halt!"

Armel was stringing his great bow; the other soldiers did the same. Each of them selected an arrow from their covered quivers.

The fog clung to the travelers as if its sole purpose was to suffocate them.

"This is their last effort," declared Madoc ap Arthus. "Believe me, I've known such strange things before, this is their last try."

The jester took out his bone pipe and began to play a gentle, haunting tune that grew louder and louder until it penetrated the mist. The wind answered its call, and slowly the mist began to curl away from the sound like water from a surfacing whale.

"It's clearing, keep playing, man!" shouted Armel. He selected his arrow and hooked it onto the string; the fog retreated farther. With one large and easy movement, he drew the bow, his left hand straight and steady, his right hand locked by his ear, his eyes searching the land ahead.

There was a startled shout. The men had not known what to expect. They were stunned to see a gigantic gray shape move through the mist, trying to keep itself hidden. Armel's bow twanged, and the shaft hummed through the clearing air like an avenging demon, straight and true for the center of the thing.

There was a crack, a splintering sound. The jester took a deep breath and returned to his piping with a frightened vigor.

The fog backed away in a widening circle. As it did so, the

travelers saw that they were entirely surrounded by the great hulking shapes. There must have been about twenty of them. At the foot of the one directly ahead lay Armel's arrow, shattered.

"By all that's marvelous," breathed Madoc.

The travelers stood agape.

"Stones!"

Yes, stones; for the shapes were rough-hewn giant stones, formed in a circle around them.

"But I saw them move!"

"And I."

"I know I saw them move, one leaped aside like a scalded cat."

There was a general murmur of agreement; they had all seen moving shapes out there.

The mist had fled entirely. The moors were clear and empty, the stones silent and cold.

Armel walked over and stared at the stone he had shot at. Then, without a word, he picked up the bent steel arrowhead and put it into his pouch. Silently he mounted his horse and gave the sign for the travelers to press onward.

18

Mabby Afraid

Every single day since Jago had left, Mabby had visited the cave. She did it carefully, under the double cover of night and her invisibility. She took great pains not to reveal her connections with those who were against the Dark Lord. Every night strange battles were being fought between the forces of the sorcerer and those few people in Penwith who still had the courage to resist.

The ferment of terror bubbled out over the land like an untended vat.

The sorcerer extended his power over the animals. Bands of crows and rooks wandered about killing any smaller birds who resisted, and in two pitched battles they overcame the sea birds and the hawks.

On the land, as well as in the air, there were savage battles, unwitnessed by the humans. Here the Dark Lord used as his soldiers ferrets, weasels, and stoats. But not even he could break the proud, independent spirit of the foxes.

Soon the evil sickness permeated the trees and grass, and the cattle, sheep, and pigs became weak and famished. The worried people turned to their leaders, but the best and truest of these men had been the first targets of the Dark Lord's scheming wrath. Their places had been taken by men of lesser worth, who gave in to the evil, or tried to appease it.

Even Mungo Trelissick, the valiant mayor of Hellys, was bewitched so that he lost his eyesight, and then the use of his mind. He was taken to the madhouse at Dunheved.

And that other loved and popular leader, the holy man of Tregony, Jowan Kea, was driven to take refuge with the good monks of Carrek Los Y'n Cos.

Every evening the sorcerer would walk on the battlements of Pengersick, and to him would fly those of his spies who had anything to report, or anyone to betray. Then he would give orders to his steward, Marek Leman, in a low, slow voice. The birds would squawk and return to their treacherous patrols, and, even as they flew away, armed men would clatter out of the gate, with huge black hounds on chains.

The country people became scared and silent. Dutifully, they carried out the sorcerer's orders and, what was worse, began to inform on each other.

Because the Trenoweths were poor and lived on stony land they were safer than most, for they had nothing worth taking. Yet they felt the sorrow and distrust that hung like smoke about the anes and fields of the country.

Mabby longed for the day when she could do something effective against the sorcerer, but she knew that for now it all depended on Jago. He had to accumulate magic power in his thorn stick, so that it could be a potent weapon to use against the Dark Lord. And for that he had to go to the Giants' Dance, to Carnac, and the Hill of Tara.

She thought of Jago all the time and prayed for his safety. How long would it be before he returned? It was a long, difficult, and dangerous journey. Mabby had been no farther than Pensans to the west and Lanvorek to the east, and could not imagine what it was like to travel in foreign countries, and especially across the sea.

One day, as she worked in the field, she heard horsemen in the lane. She looked up and saw Marek Leman in the company of the sorcerer and three soldiers. Marek carried a small wax tablet and a stylus.

"Hey, there," he called. "Trenoweth?"

"Yes, what's that to you?" answered Mabby sharply, although she was shaking inside.

"Taxes, that's what."

"We pay no land tax. This is our own property."

"But you pay common tax."

"Yes, Father pays common tax to the mayor of Hellys."

"I am the new mayor of Hellys. Next quarter day your tax will be paid to me in Hellys market."

They were about to ride off when the sorcerer frowned and held up his hand.

"Hold it, Leman. I remember this girl, she tried to defy me once. She's got spirit. Hey, girl, can you cook? Can you sew?"

"I can do anything I want to do."

His piercing black eyes gleamed. "Can you sing, girl? Can you plait hair and do fine needlework?"

"I can, sir, if need be. I was maid to the Lady of Germoe before she died. Why, I can read books as well!"

"And now you wield a hoe instead of a comb? Would you like to live in a castle, girl, eat dainty food and wear rich clothes?"

"I would, if the company were right."

The man leaned back and laughed.

"Perhaps, my girl, there might be a chance of that. If my lady likes you, you will come to us."

"Will I, sir?"

"I said 'if.' "

"And I said 'Will I?' I do not go where I am told, only where I want to."

"Oh, we shall see about that, young defiance! There's a lout or two in my gatehouse could teach you better manners with a birch rod! We shall see."

Marek Leman was angry. "My lord, shall I give the girl a good thrashing now for her impudence?"

"No, Marek, no, I'll break her when I want to. Come, I'm expecting those visitors."

"Those stinking moor men? Ach, I tell you, my lord, they fair make my guts turn!"

"If they have succeeded, then they will be rewarded, no matter how foul they stink."

With that they whipped their horses and rode off.

Mabby's mind whirled. What was that about a lady at Pengersick Castle? And who were the moor men? Jago had to cross a moor; could it be that the sorcerer knew he had escaped from the mine? And was he now trying to stop Jago? Mabby trembled with fear; she felt dreadfully alone. What if Jago did not return at all? What if she were left to fight by herself?

19

Giants' Dance

As they approached Sarum Hill, all the travelers began to
sing, and the jester sang loudest of all. It was a song full of
warmth and happiness. A song of gratitude. To Jago it was like
waking up on a summer morning after a night of storm. They
began to pass other travelers, on foot and horseback, and droves
of cattle and slow-creaking farm carts, piled high with good
things.

The soldiers took off their helmets and beat time to the song
with the handles of their daggers.

At a bend in the road, the plain came into view. To one side
rose the hill of Sarum, with smoke rising from the huddled
houses of the town. The tents for the fair made the grass white.

"Look, Jago lad, feast your ignorant Kernow eyes. That's
Sarum, heigh-ho for the Goose Fair. Good things to drink, good
things to eat, boy! Songs, strange people and animals from overseas. Spotted leopards and giant snakes, harpers and jugglers,
and pretty girls with dancing feet! Hooray for Sarum Fair!"

"Gold-a-jingle in our purses on the homeward journey,"
said the kind merchant, smiling. "New shoes and a bright new
gown for my wife."

"Good bow staves, too," said Armel to his men. "Sharp arrows and fine blades. And the horses! Leather work from
Treglas, saddles fit for a king, bridles fit for the horses of the
sun itself!"

"Aye, boy," said the jester, smiling with his whole body. "That's Sarum Fair. Hey, boy?"

But Jago had gone.

The jester turned and would have followed, but at a look from Armel he stopped.

Jago stood by the side of the road as the cavalcade of fair-goers passed by, but he seemed not to notice them: the men from far countries, the sea-bronzed sailors, the soldiers, the merchants, herdsmen, peasants, musicians, tinkers, peddlers, gypsies, and serfs. Nor did he seem to notice the lush valley, the white tents and pavilions beneath the green trees, the clustered walls and roofs of Sarum.

Jago gazed at the horizon, toward the blue edge of the Great Plain, where the Giants' Dance stood in perpetual stone. His heart was thumping loudly, his cheeks and ears burned, his throat felt dry, and there was a stinging feeling in his eyes.

The road branched and Jago turned left down the hill. Everyone else followed the path straight ahead to Sarum.

Jago found himself on an empty gravel track, leading northwest. After walking for two hours, he saw in the distance what he thought was a line of men in gray cloaks. He shaded his eyes, and realized that they were not men but stones.

It was a stone avenue. Beyond it, he saw a double circle of massive monoliths. From where he stood, the temple, which was what it was, did indeed look like a group of giants frozen in the middle of a round dance.

As he drew closer, Jago could make out groups of men wandering aimlessly about the vast structure. They were all dressed alike in white homespun robes with hoods.

Soon he was walking down the stone avenue. It was so constructed that from the path one got the impression that the walls on either side were solid. The effect of this illusion was to concentrate one's vision on the temple ahead.

"Off with your shoes, young man," said a voice.

Looking around, Jago saw an old man with a wispy white beard. He had a smiling face and carried a bowl of water. Jago did as he was bid, and to his surprise the old man began to wash his dusty feet.

"Wait, what are you doing?"

The old man merely smiled.

"There's no need . . ."

"Need? What is water for then? Other foot up!" With nimble fingers the old man dried Jago's feet. Jago had to admit it felt refreshing.

"Come on," said whitebeard, and led the way down the avenue.

"Leave your weapons here," said another voice. It belonged to a second man who suddenly appeared from behind a stone.

Jago took out his flint knife and offered it to the man, who drew back sharply in surprise. The first old man chuckled.

"You see, you never believe anything until it happens, you weak fool," he cackled.

"I . . . I . . ."

"Oh, shut up, and get out of our way. Don't you worry about him, boy. He doesn't know anything. Been here thirty years, and still as pig-ignorant as ever. Can't calculate solstices, can't remember his epic poems, can't recite Gwyon's riddles, can't compose treaties, can't even remember his own wretched ancestry. Tsk, tsk, tsk. What will happen to our knowledge with pupils like him? Can't get young men nowadays, not the clever ones. Well, and how is the dear old land of Kernow, eh?"

"Nyns-yu 'vas," said Jago.

"Drok yu genef," replied the old man.

They walked on a bit. The old man sniffed.

"I hoped I wouldn't live to see this day, but I'm proud to be of any help."

Jago smiled nervously and cleared his throat. To tell the truth, he was a little worried by this old man with his high-pitched voice, slightly mad eyes, and knowledge of Kernewek. Could he have had the bad luck to fall in with the temple idiot?

The old man cackled again. He acted as if he had been expecting Jago. Then, without warning, he started to make a brassy, braying sound. Jago was even more worried and embarrassed, and looked about anxiously, hoping that the noise would not attract too much attention from the priests.

Jago had worked hard to reach this, the first stage in his magical journey. Now he felt cheated. Where was the solemn ceremony attended by grave-faced soothsayers and magi? Why was he stuck with this addle-brained nitwit?

"Look, thank you for your help, but I can find my own way," he said to the old man.

"No you can't, but I knew you would say that."

"Why . . . I mean how?"

"Because I've studied this event closely. I know what's going to happen, word for word."

"Do you?"

"There you are. What did I tell you, word for word."

"Show me where to stand."

The old man smiled. They had now penetrated to the very center of the huge stone circle and passed under a great trilithon.

"Wait here! Attend, ye guardians! The hour has come when time must be pinned by the ears to the tree of will. If you see what I mean," squeaked the old man. In the enclosed space his voice carried like a trumpet in a cave.

Jago bit his lip in shame, especially when he noticed that before each space and stone there had appeared a venerable white-haired elder. He fidgeted, and leaned on his thorn stick. He felt sleepy; a rushing sound filled his ears. He was looking at himself from high in the sky, looking down through a long, black tube. There he was, right at the bottom, a tiny figure in a toy temple.

A fierce ray of sunshine splashed onto a rock.

"Now, don't fail!" said a voice.

Jago was back in his body again; something solid slithered over his foot. He glanced down and saw a salamander, a bright lizard with a skin as thickly jeweled as a crown, making for the spot where the sun glowed on the rock.

His instinct took over. He lunged forward with his stick and hit the patch of sunlight a fraction before the salamander could get there.

"Aaah!" he cried. His whole body jerked and shook as the force of the sun was sucked into the stick. The salamander rolled over and shriveled up.

The old man laughed and danced like a maniac.

The violence of the event subsided; everything returned to normal. It was as if nothing had happened, nothing at all. The men in white robes wandered off about their business, un-hurried and unperturbed.

Jago trembled. Some incomprehensible deep power had entered the stick; he felt it vibrate. Outwardly it was still the same as before, just an ordinary thorn stick. But Jago could feel its new potency.

The foolish old man looked into Jago's eyes, and was worried by what he saw there.

"Surely you knew what would happen? You are an initiate of the Way, are you not?"

"I knew nothing at all, really," replied Jago.

Before the old man could continue, they were joined by some-one else.

"Your journey is not over," said a wise, friendly voice. Jago saw a tall, magical figure standing nearby. At last, someone of authority and bearing!

"So I believe, sir. I have only just started."

"Take this to help you." The tall man offered Jago a gold coin.

"Please excuse me, sir. I cannot accept."

"Oh, but please. I promise you it will be helpful."

"No, but thank you very much. I do appreciate your desire to help but—"

"I insist, dear boy, you have a hard journey ahead. You have achieved much to come this far. Go on, take it."

"I don't think I should."

"Be careful, boy," muttered the foolish oldster.

"Who are you to tell me to be careful?" retorted Jago.

"Take it," said the tall man. An edge of command had crept into his voice.

"No, sir."

"Take it! Damn your eyes, take the coin!" The tall man shook with fury. He threw the gold piece at Jago and turned about imperiously.

With a shout, Jago bent and picked up the coin. It was hot. He flung it back. Even if the man was someone in authority, Jago wasn't going to be pushed about.

The coin hit the tall man in the back, between the shoulder blades. It tore through the woolen robe and sank deep into his flesh. The man gave a shriek and collapsed. It was like a balloon being punctured: his body seemed to cave in with a hiss of outward-rushing air, until he lay in a crumpled heap no bigger than a robe. The heap moved, and out of the folds of the garment appeared a large, sooty crow with red eyes. It gave a great wringing cry of sorrow, and flew off.

Jago looked bitterly at the retreating bird and said, "Even here, in this holy place, even here! Who are you?"

He turned accusingly on the giggling old man who had been watching the drama, apparently quite unmoved.

"Ah, boy, if only you knew. But how did you get caught up in all this, if you haven't looked ahead? That means you've jumped clean over the first ten years' work and are trying the journey straight off. Well I never."

"You mean to tell me that you foresaw all this?"

Jago realized that the man was speaking the truth. He understood now that the idiotic behavior was only an act: that beneath the humble exterior of the foot washer and guide was an important and powerful person indeed. He felt very small and foolish.

"You've taken the first step, take more soon. Get to know the adventures of the spirit. That's the way to master magic. As they say in Kernow, Dew genough-why!"

"Durdala-dhywhy!" replied Jago.

20

Sunbeam and Song

Jago traveled south with speed. It seemed to him that he had at last reached the real beginning of his journey. The miles passed. The incidents along the route merged into one long pleasant show, which he watched as unconcernedly as if it had been a puppet play. Things that once would have seemed amusing or vivid now no longer affected him. He just smiled and passed by.

He reached a seaport. The water was crammed with boats, some big enough to carry horses, most just the right size for a small crew and enough merchandise to make a coastal journey profitable. There were skin boats just big enough for two men, trim little sailing boats with open tops, and one or two dumpy scows with simple planking laid over dark holds. Others were frail river boats, drawing no more than a few inches of water.

The place was called Porthgwyn and hid in a cleft in the white chalk cliffs. As Jago approached, he stopped to drink at a small stream; the water had a slight fishy taste. In the port, he paused outside a low cottage. There was a one-legged man drawing something on a sheet of parchment. Around him other skins were drying, stretched tight on frames hung up in the sun.

The man had a bundle of reed pens and a pot of ink. He was carefully tracing an outline on the skin. Jago stood and watched. The man looked up and smiled.

"Welcome. How is the road today?"

"As ever, stony and unending."

"But the same?"

"Yes, the same."

"Out there is another road. A road that's never the same. I mean the sea. I traveled on that road for many a year. And though I never set foot upon it, yet I lost my leg through journeying thereon." The man laughed gently at his own misfortune.

"How did you lose it?"

"Oh, a sea monster bit it off. But I killed the beast with a harpoon. My shipmates opened its belly and found my leg. You know, the juices of its guts had bleached that leg of mine white? Whiter than that of the fairest maid on Severnside. And I should know, by all the gods and little fishes!" And he laughed again, having to stop work until his mirth subsided.

"Oh, dearie me, what days, what days!"

"You were a mariner?" asked Jago.

The man nodded. He turned his head to show the gold ring piercing his ear, and pulled up his sleeve, exposing black spidery tattoo marks on his arm.

"See, both of them charms against the sea spirits. Perhaps if I'd had my leg tattooed it wouldn't have got bit off."

"Are there ships leaving the harbor today?"

"Today? It's plain to see you're a land sailor. No offense. No, the wind's onshore and the rip tide's running strong. No sailor will haul a rope till tomorrow midday by the smell of the wind. Unless he wants to leave tonight. You come from a terrible coast."

"Me?"

"From Kernow, right? Knew it by your slow speech and your swarthy looks. Good sailors come from that land. And good wrecks end there. Aye, I've been locked in the bays of Kernow by that dreadful wind, praying not to hit the rocks. Where are you seeking passage?"

"Bretan Vyghan."

"Ah."

"You know of a ship going there?"

"You have money?"

"No, but I can work, and cook, and sing, and tend horses."

"No horses on the sea, cold food only, no time for singing. But you can work?"

"Yes, as well as any other man."

"Oh, it's a man you are, then?"

"Is there a ship?"

"Now look, I've a thought. Take this chart, new-drawn and fresh-dried, down to the haven and ask for a ship named *Sunbeam*. Give the chart to Emlyn Dubhgall and tell him your desires. And watch out for sea monsters."

Jago took the chart; it smelt of ink and gall and pumice. He walked down to the harbor, where he soon found the ship. It seemed larger than most. It was very old and had two masts and six oars. It stank of fish and oil and lay on the water like a sad, abandoned frog.

"Sir!" called Jago, when he glimpsed some movement under the half-decking. "Is Emlyn Dubhgall there?"

The sailor stood up. He was tall and lean and dark, with a hooked nose and a scar on his forehead. He nodded. Jago wondered what to do; he had never been on a ship before. Was he expected to leap the two yards of sea onto the gently moving deck? Or would the man come over to him?

The sailor just stood and looked. Jago drew a deep breath and leaped onto the deck. He went across to the man and gave him the chart.

"Good," said the sailor, gazing at the chart appreciatively. He rolled it up and tied it with a thong. Then he looked at Jago.

"I want to go to Bretan Vyghan," said Jago.

"A passenger?"

Jago laughed; he held out his hands.

"With these, although they are empty."

"Can you swim, then?"

"I can learn, but I want to get there faster than that."

"Can you work with ropes?"

"I catch ponies, I can tie any knot there is."

"Tie me a fast knot that will hold a man, which he can release from the other end of the rope." The sailor tossed Jago a thick cord and pointed to the yardarm.

Jago took off his cloak, placed it on the deck with his stick, and climbed nimbly up the mast. He tied a double slip knot and used the rope to slide down on. The sailor pulled hard at the rope and swung on it; then he tugged at the other end and the knot loosened. The rope fell to the deck.

"Now for something easy. Just tie this rope to the mast, on this spot. Tie it so it doesn't slip."

It was quite a problem; the mast's surface had been worn slippery by generations of sailors. Jago fastened the rope swiftly and easily. The sailor was pleased.

"I'm lacking a crew this trip. We've ten pigs to take as well; the beasts need tying and keeping quiet. I'll take you."

"Thank you, thank you. I'll start on that lot." Jago pointed to a mess of rope that needed sorting and coiling.

Emlyn Dubhgall smiled. He wandered off humming a discordant melody.

Early next morning the pigs came aboard, closely followed by the rest of the crew. The sailors had been drinking heavily in the taverns of Porthgwyn. It was difficult to tell them apart from the animals, especially as they collapsed among the swine and immediately fell asleep.

"Ah, home in the bosom of their family," said Emlyn. He didn't seem to mind too much, and he and Jago cast off and took the *Sunbeam* out of the harbor alone. Emlyn said little, but when the old ship left the sheltered waters and hit into the wind and open sea, he became a changed man. His face and body glowed with new life. He stood on the deck, with one hand on the steering beam, and was part of the ship. The *Sunbeam* ran before the wind like a greyhound; Jago's first impression of her in the harbor had been quite mistaken.

Toward noon, Emlyn allowed Jago to take over the steering. He fetched apples, honey, and bread.

"Hold her straight, lad."

"How long will it take us?"

"With this wind we shall be out of the narrow seas by sunset. Then we turn south around the first headland, past the islands, and down to Brieuc. Who knows, if we get a good passage, maybe we'll sight Brieuc tomorrow morning. I'm off to sleep."

"Sleep?"

"Yes, sleep, you just keep her head where it is."

And with that he spat out an apple pip, wrapped himself in a striped blanket, and curled up in a corner.

Jago realized that everyone on the boat was asleep except himself and the pigs, who were grunting and snuffling among themselves. He should have felt worried, but the old boat with her creaking sails leaped through the sea like an eager pony, and like a good mount she seemed to know her way. About him were the limitless sea and the sun and, in his hair and the sails, the cold, clean wind. Jago tasted contentment; now he understood both the reserved silence of Emlyn and the gusty laughter of the one-legged chart maker, whom he remembered having said, "If you are fond of the sea, no monster can really hurt you. So what if you lose a leg or an arm? They can't bite off your happiness with it."

And so the *Sunbeam* shone through the sea. After a few more miles, one of the sailors awoke, dashed some water in his face from the barrel by the mast, and approached Jago.

"It's my trick now, youngster." He yawned, and took the helm. Jago looked over the side; the sailor watched him.

"Not wanting to sleep? Hey, is that your cloak? I've heard of you from a mate of mine. Were you not on the road to Sarum a short while back?"

"There were a lot of us on that road."

"True, but I heard tell of a boy in a wolfskin cloak who out-fought the moor men."

"Many people wear wolfskin cloaks," replied Jago.

"Also true. What do men call you?"

"My name is Jago Blythcroghan."

"You're the lad all right. Saucy and bold, they said. Yes, a mate of mine traveled with you. What did you think of the wild men? My mate said you had a magic knife."

"I had no magic knife. This is the one I used, an old flint knife, a good deal cheaper than metal."

"And no rust. But a bold lad like you should get a decent cut-lass, there's money to be made by turning soldier. Loot, rich pickings . . . Another mate of mine went for a freebooter. Set himself up for life in three voyages."

"He became a pirate?"

"Aye, that's the right word. I tell you, sometimes I'm tempted. But Emlyn's a good captain, treats a man fair and civil. I've no complaints. If I had to ship with some captains you see nowa-days, I'd as lief slit their throats as I would a herring's belly. Emlyn's got a new ship building, see, and I'm to take care of the good old *Sunbeam*. I'll be a captain myself next moon. This is Emlyn's last voyage in the old ship."

The sailor reached for the bread that Emlyn had left by the tiller, and cut himself a hunk with a large, sharp knife.

"Can you sing, lad? There's my harp in that locker there. Give us a song to make the ship fly faster."

Jago found the harp in the locker and tried it. It was old and some of its strings were not true. He hummed and tuned it by turning the bone pegs until the sound was right.

He sang a song he had learned from the fishermen on Marghas Yow Sands. The ship seemed to give a great sigh of

pleasure and picked up speed. Emlyn murmured in his sleep.
The other two sailors woke up and sat listening quietly.

The helmsman started on another song, and Jago joined in
with the harp until it and the man's voice blended as one. It
was a song of the coasters in the Celtic Sea:

Where are the lads who sailed with me
Last summer over the sunny sea
From Pensans path to Shannon Lee,
Bosinney Cove to Bal Naree?

Where are the lads who sailed with me
Last winter over the frosty sea
From Barra Head to Marghas Yow,
Where are they now?

Oh, some sleep in Morwenstowe,
Lodenek graves and old Mayo,
And on their bones the grasses grow
And through their ribs the south winds blow.

While I go sailing,
Sailing, sailing,
Sailing still upon the sea.
From Syllan reefs to Loighaire strand.

Their bones lie scattered with the sand
And I go sailing,
Sailing, sailing,
Sailing still upon the sea.

The plaintive song died away, and Jago saw in the glow of
the setting sun that the singer, the man whose harp he was
playing, held the tiller awkwardly. He had not noticed it before,
but the man had three fingers missing from his hand. So that
was why the harp was untuned!

"Boy," said the man quietly, "that old harp has fallen into
good hands at last. I want you to keep it and play it and give

people pleasure with your playing. It would be unkind to let it remain silent."

Jago replied by playing the harp again, a rousing tune that had the sailors beating time. But in spite of the general merriment he could not help noticing a tear run down the man's cheek.

21

The Second Pattern

Before they reached the coast, Jago cut up some old sailcloth and sewed a cover for the harp.

After helping to unload the pigs, he ate a last meal of apples and honey with Emlyn and the sailors and walked south, inland, making for the headland where Carnac stood.

It was an easy and pleasant journey, and Jago found to his delight that the people spoke a language almost identical to Kernewek. He was able to ask his way and find work in return for food. Sooner than he had hoped, he was leaning on his thorn stick looking down on Carnac.

Jago had not known what to expect, certainly nothing like this. Marching across the countryside in regular ranks were hundreds upon hundreds of huge, upright stones. He could see no beginning and no end to the procession.

For more than an hour, Jago just stood and stared at this astonishing sight. Then, trembling with excitement, he descended the hill, and was soon among the great monoliths.

It was like being in an enormous stone wood; whichever way he turned, it looked the same. Jago walked and walked; the grass between the stones was thick and springy. There were large, fat sheep grazing, but no sign of a shepherd, or anyone else who could direct him.

The sky had darkened; heavy, black clouds rolled overhead.

Jago hoped it would not rain; he was concerned for his harp in its thin sailcloth cover.

He heard children's voices and eventually came upon a small group of them, squatting by a flat stone. They were playing jacks with a handful of sheep's knuckle bones. He sat down to watch, and placed his stick against another, larger stone.

The bones rattled and the children yelled and laughed.

"Did you kill that wolf yourself? With a spear?" asked one of them.

"I killed it with an ax," said Jago.

"Let me see it," demanded the small boy.

"I left it at home. Where's the shepherd?"

"We look after the sheep," said the boy. "We don't have wolves here. Do you come from Frynk?"

"No, from Kernow."

"You speak strangely. Want a throw?"

"Thanks," said Jago. He took the bones. "This is how we rattle them in Kernow," he said, moving his clasped hands quickly so that the bones clattered. He stopped, for at that moment a deep growl had come from the clouds. The children looked up in alarm.

"We've got to go."

"No, wait for your bones."

"We've got to go," said the boy, and sped away, followed silently by the others.

Jago shrugged and threw the bones onto the flat stone.

There are many ways of throwing bones, and you can go on throwing them until your hair turns white, getting a different pattern each time. Most of the patterns have absolutely no significance, but there are three that are very special indeed. Only two of these three patterns have been thrown in the whole history of the game.

The First Pattern was the original one to be thrown. The

Third Pattern hasn't been thrown yet. But the Second Pattern was the one thrown by Jago Blythcroghan at Carnac, when the bones stopped rolling and lay still. The ground quaked, the stones trembled, the air bubbled. A clap of thunder burst out and a searing flash of lightning darted down and hit the top of Jago's thorn stick. Some of the power spilled onto the stone against which the stick rested, turning the solid rock into glass, into a vitreous crust a foot wide. But most of the magic slipped, without any apparent reaction, into the stick itself.

Then it rained: huge, violent raindrops, each big enough to fill a snail shell. Jago grabbed the stick and ran off among the stones, looking for a way out. He emerged into the open countryside and threw himself into a ditch. The stick was still warm.

The force of the rain at last moved the bones, breaking up the pattern, and almost at once the weather cleared.

Jago got up and walked over to a group of stunted trees, trying to find a dry spot to sit on. He was shaking with tiredness and guilt, as if he were to blame for what had happened. He realized that his throwing the bones had triggered off something important, although he knew nothing of the Three Patterns and their significance.

What he did know was that there could be no turning back from the path he had chosen; that he had come very near to something that transcended death itself; and that magic was dangerous. It was no game.

Exhausted, yet full of desperate resolve to press on, he slumped under one of the trees. He pulled his wolfskin cloak close about him and drifted into a long slumber.

22

The Raising of Guland

Marek Leman was puzzled. For at least a week now his master, the Lord of Pengersick, had not gone out hunting in the woods or on the moor. Nor had he waded the marshes of Cober and Trevaylor with bow or otter spear. He had kept close to himself in the upper part of his tower, had eaten nothing but vegetables and fruit, had drunk nothing but water. All day and all night he read the heavy pages of his books, or tramped the battlements in thought, or stared into the depths of his crystal.

Today he had ordered Leman to prepare hot water for a bath and had spent an hour or so washing. After the servants had removed the copper tub and the piles of damp towels, he ordered them not to disturb him until he rang.

Leman was frightened. He had smelled strange incense on the stairs and had heard his master muttering to himself in a voice that was scarcely human. He knew that the Dark Lord dabbled in strange practices, but today he felt uncomfortable as never before.

He went to the stables and then to the kennels, pretending to check that all was in order—but his real reason was to see how the animals were reacting. He knew that animals often sensed the uncanny. He was right, they were all restless. All, that is, except the sorcerer's big black stallion. He remained calm while the others rolled their eyes, pricked up their ears, and tugged at their fodder. The dogs were in a similar state. They were awed into silence, but their eyes were bright with expectation.

Leman walked out toward the tall pines that bordered the castle. It was several minutes before he realized that all the crows, choughs, and rooks were silent. Never had there been such forbidding atmosphere at Pengersick.

"Leman, hey, Leman. The Master wants you!" It was one of the guards, his face white, his voice troubled. "You're to go straight up!"

Leman hurried up the gloomy staircase and tapped on the wide oaken door.

"Marek? Come in, and fasten the door behind you."

Leman's jaw fell in surprise. He didn't recognize the room. The walls were covered with a rich damask he had never seen before; the rugs and furs had been piled in a corner, revealing the marbled floor inlaid with cabalistic signs.

The sorcerer was garbed in a simple white gown, hooded and girdled. His eyes seemed to have sunk into his flesh like diamonds into mud, and they burned with a bright fire. Heavy perfume from smoking burners filled the room with mist. A small open casket full of what appeared to be black earth stood on a table in front of him.

"Step forward, Marek, don't be alarmed. Answer me clearly. You are Marek Leman?"

"Yes, my lord."

"You are thirty years old and were born on the stroke of midnight in the valley of Nancegollan?"

"Yes, but how did you know?"

"I ask the question. You have a scar on your left shoulder made by a spade? And a birthmark on your left arm?"

"Yes."

"You are the son of Trevern Leman of Nancegollan?"

"Yes."

"You are accused of killing a friend, Saul Chegwidden?"

"It was an accident—"

"You killed Chegwidden for the sake of a girl?"

Leman stepped backward.

"Answer!"

"Yes, it's no good lying to you, you seem to know it all anyway. But how?"

"Listen, Marek Leman, I know everything about you, even things that have not yet happened. You have been a good steward. I have already made you mayor of Hellys in my name. I now wish to thank you by giving you real power. The gift comes in two parts. First, I give you and yours the manor of Marghas Yow, with all rights over the market and the lands from there to Gulval and back again to Perran Uthnoe, to use as you think fit. Secondly, I will give you the honor of helping me, to witness before the spirits what passes here this night. Do you agree to this willingly and with no compulsion?"

"I do, my lord, most willingly."

"Good. Now come and stand in this circle and hand me my implements as I ask for them. Do not fail and do not fear."

Trembling a little, Leman stepped into the circle. It was not bad after all. Indeed he felt stronger and more relaxed than he had for a long time. Perhaps it was the perfume.

The sorcerer began to speak, with difficulty, as if there were a heavy weight on his chest. Picking up the casket from the table, he sprinkled black earth in a circle around them. When the circle was complete, he set the casket down and began to sway, muttering strange words. Occasionally he would make abrupt gestures with his arms or with his whole body. Leman got the impression that he was helping the sorcerer by just being there, as if his strength were somehow being absorbed and diverted.

Leman felt strangely light-headed. He giggled to himself and was just about to make a silly comment when Pengersick threw out his arms and called loudly, "O Guland, I conjure and adjure thee in the name of Sathanas and Beelzebub, and in the name of Astaroth, and in the names of all other spirits! Do thou come instantly before me! Come now in these names and the names of all the demons. Come, I order thee, in the name of the most Holy Three. Come without injury to me, my body, my soul, my books, or anything of mine, including my servant here, Marek Leman, who is mine, body, breath, and soul. I order thee to manifest thyself at once. Otherwise thou mayest dispatch unto me some other spirit, empowered to act equally as thee, acting on my orders and subject to the conditions above. And he should not be licensed to leave this spot until he has done my bidding!"

The smoke in the room began to thicken and take shape. The walls and the roof melted and disappeared. To Leman, standing inside the circle, it was like being on a tiny platform on the edge of nothing; the drop into blackness was terrifying. A great wind began to blow among the stars that were shining all about, but all so far away, so small.

Out of the mist in front of them a gigantic figure slowly emerged, towering above the stars. As the figure became clearer, Leman saw with horror and disgust that it was composed of thousands of little colored shapes, some like animals he knew, some like foul monsters or nightmare demons, some like shining snakes, some like humans. They were in constant movement, in endless twisted battle, as they chased, fought, devoured, and regurgitated each other. Hundreds of teeth flashed, hundreds of evil eyes glinted through the billowing smoke and dripping blood—like a universe of maggots feeding on a huge corpse.

Leman fell to his knees.

"Get up!" screamed the sorcerer. "Do not kneel to him, he is our servant. Guland! Tell me, where is the Black Sigil of Pengersick, where is my ring? And what is this force that makes me stammer? What is this force that suffuses my heart with pain?"

A deep, penetrating voice rumbled from the other side of creation.

"O Master, O mighty one of Pengersick, Lord of Thought, the ring you seek is hidden in your heart. The force that tries to strangle your words is the most frightful and powerful of all."

"That is no answer! Speak fast or I strike."

"Pity, Master, pity. I am too weak."

"Where is the ring? What is the force? Marek, hand me the sword!"

Leman picked up the glistening blade; it shone eagerly. He handed it to the sorcerer.

"Mercy, mercy."

"Fool!" shrieked the Dark Lord, and lunged forward. The giant cowered as the sword seemed to grow, to leap up and slice into the gross, bubbling body.

"You have no right to treat me like this, no right, no right."

The sword flashed again and the giant burst. A shower of crying demons, rotten flesh, foul liquid, rats, and ghouls spilt out in a grotesque flood.

A thin despairing voice cried out, "Curse you, Pengersick, may you melt in hell! It is love that chokes you!"

Pengersick's eyes flashed. "Tell me, tell me!" he demanded.

The apparition gasped and threw up its monstrous head. "You have stolen away the lifeblood of your Lord. You have misused your power, so you hunger for greater power. It was your fault that your lady lies there in that box, one of the living dead. For love of her you are seeking to uncover hidden power, and you do not care who stands in your way. It is too late, the reaction to your ways has already begun! Beware, beware the power of innocence. Beware the strength of the meek!"

The figure twisted and struggled for a moment, then collapsed and disappeared, leaving smoke curling about the room.

Leman blinked; the walls, floor, and roof had returned, solid as ever. Time began to flow again. Everything was back to normal. He prepared to step out of the circle. The sorcerer held him back.

"Not yet, Marek: my scepter."

Leman handed it to him and the Dark Lord made the movements of banishing.

"You can step out now."

"Sir, what was that smoke?" Already the conscious memory of the spirit was fading from Leman's mind.

The sorcerer rubbed his hands together in savage satisfaction. "I gave that fiend something to remember. It will not easily forget who its master is. Well, now for the contract."

He strolled over to a stand and opened a huge book. He scribbled in it. A wry smile covered his face.

"Sign here, Marek. Good, now a drop of your blood to seal it."

Leman looked on calmly as the sorcerer took a bodkin and pricked his thumb for him. He felt no pain; the spot of blood on the page looked very small.

"Congratulations, Marek Leman, Lord of Marghas Yow."

"Thank you, my lord. As you know, things are not too good over there. Those interfering monks from the mount are to blame. Now I'm their lord, I'll put paid to the lot of them. You see if I don't."

"Good, I'm very pleased. I'll help. You had better leave. I think you'll find your horse is ready."

"What, now?"

"Yes, now. And remember, not a word about today."

"Of course not."

Pengersick smiled, a wicked smile. "Or else the demon will come and cut your heart out."

Leman began to tremble violently. The sorcerer looked deep into his eyes to calm him.

"I'll visit you soon. Good luck!"

Leman walked down from the tower in a daze. He pushed past the guards, mounted the horse that was waiting, and rode as fast as he could from Pengersick. No one saw him ride. If they had they would have stood aside in fear, for his skin was yellow, his lips purple, and his blood-shot eyes revealed the hopelessness of a lost soul.

23

Pirates

The dark conjurations of the Lord of Pengersick seemed to drift over the countryside like a plague, leaving a trail of sickness and despair. Something of the sickness was blown away by the fierce winds, but then shreds of it were carried far and wide until the winds themselves became tainted.

Jago, standing by the mast of the trader, raised his face to the wind. It was from the land of Kernow, but it tasted foul; as evil as Pengersick. He had been on board for three days and his quiet efficiency had impressed the captain, a cheery Breton, who left Jago alone to steer the ship at night.

"Just keep the star to your right hand and watch for white water."

They were carrying bales of woolen cloth and fat pigs of iron to the West Islands—the captain called them Enesow Spycys, Spice Islands. He was forever talking about them and their exotic plants.

"And when we load up with sweet spice and rich barks we're off to the land of Ywerdhon. The King of Sianion always pays good red gold for spices. It is the land of Ywerdhon you wish to go to, lad?"

Jago spent the evenings and nights playing on his harp. Whenever he picked it up and drew his hand over the strings, a deep feeling of joy took hold of his mind. The harp would grow warm and easy to play. Jago remembered all the songs and words he had heard; his fingers flew to the strings of their own accord without his having to think.

And so the ship sailed on before the gentle wind, and the sea echoed to Jago's songs.

During the day he would put the harp into its sailcloth cover, wrap himself in his cloak, and sleep on the deck.

It was the fact that he slept there, with his cheek against his harp, that saved his life. For as the Spice Islands came in sight, a pirate galley sprang upon the trading vessel like a greyhound upon a rabbit. Sleek and lean, the pirate ship raced up before she was spotted and overhauled the trader. With hooks and lines the pirates grappled the merchant, and the captain wisely surrendered. It would have been foolishness to fight.

The pirates, concerned by the fierce wolfskin worn by Jago, were all for plunging a sword into his throat as he slept. But their leader, Cumail Conan, noticed the harp in its cover and bade them put up their blades.

"Sure 'tis no great warrior but a lad, and a singer, too. He'll fetch a better price in the slave market than these dumb oxen. As for the wolfskin, it looks so mangy I imagine it was some beast trapped by his doddering grandsire."

"I'm after trying the harp," said a young, merry-eyed pirate, named Hiernan.

Cumail Conan nodded, and Hiernan swiftly pulled the harp away so that Jago's sleeping head thudded onto the deck. He woke with a jerk and stared at the ring of grinning, bearded faces.

The captain's miserable expression, the rough appearance of the pirates, and their bright blades gave him enough clues to what had happened.

Hiernan uncovered the harp and tried the strings.

"Pah, it's an ill-made frame. Stiff and unwieldy, like an unwilling maid. It has no soul." He ran his ringed hands down the strings. "It's an imitation of a harp, a fit instrument for a Kernow peasant." And he shook his head sneeringly.

"It's a good harp, begging your pardon," said Jago.

But he was ignored. The pirates had turned their attention to sorting out the goods on the ship. They were already arguing about who should have what. Jago realized that they would not use force unless provoked.

"What will happen to us?" he asked the captain.

"They'll make us sail with them back to Ywerdhon. They'll sell the ship and us, too. But we will have our lives."

"That's all I've got anyway."

The captain looked at Jago's possessions: his clothes, pouch, flint knife, and thorn stick. Even the harp, his only tangible wealth, was old and chipped. The pirates, their own harps inlaid with gold and silver, laughed at it.

"Dermot, you're in charge here," said Cumail Conan. "You will account to us in six weeks when we return. Perhaps we will even be there before you, if our luck holds."

Dermot and three pirates remained on the Breton ship, while the others returned to their slim vessel.

"What a beautiful sight," said Jago, as the pirate craft sped off to the west.

"As beautiful and as cruel as the ice princess," said Dermot.

"Steer north, Kernow peasant, I'll tell you the way to Lifi."

And so he did. It all seemed very strange. They went about their tasks exactly as before. Only the constant presence of the armed pirates, and their new course, told them they were now slaves.

At last they reached a low, green coast. The pirates were on edge; they paced the decks while looking worriedly at the horizon.

"More speed, more speed," called Dermot. He had spotted

approaching ships. The old merchant vessel rolled sluggishly in the water, and the other craft gained with each sea mile.

"Speed this old bucket up, sir," shouted Dermot to the Breton captain. "Those are the ships of the High King."

With that he drew his sword.

"You are not on your galloping battle steed now, but on a plodding old pack horse," answered the captain bravely. "We cannot go faster."

"You can go faster than this. What's holding us up?"

The captain shrugged. He caught Jago's eye and managed to suppress a look of triumph. It was strange that the ship was not making more headway. They had crowded up every inch of canvas and yet she still dragged and rolled like a log.

The King's ships were within hailing distance, and the pirates were in despair. They drew their swords and got ready to make a fight of it. They realized that they were trapped; the other ships were preparing boarders.

"Give up," said Jago. "You can't win."

"We have a code of honor. We'll die fighting. I was born free and will remain so. I do not fear death but slavery. I have royal blood in my veins," said Dermot proudly.

"Oh, it's not so bad being a slave," said Jago.

Dermot laughed. "You have a sense of humor for a Kernow peasant. It's a pity you were not born to honor. Watch me and learn how a man of breeding dies!"

The King's soldiers swarmed aboard. It was madness. The four pirates went boldly forward and there was a short and bloody fight. One by one, they were cut down. They asked no mercy and were shown none. Only Dermot was left, and then he fell in a slippery pool of blood.

From the deck he looked up at Jago.

"Goodbye, boy. Good riddance to your slow old ship."

"You were wrong about the ship, she's fast, she could have outrun these saviors of ours."

"How?" coughed Dermot.

"Remember we were carrying iron? Well, we made a sea anchor of our spare sail and weighted it with the stuff to keep it under water. Look, there's the rope right under your nose." He pointed to a rope tied securely to the stern.

Dermot's face turned black. "I die an honorable death," he said. There was silence.

The King's men looked on in amazement as Jago and the Breton captain dragged the sea anchor aboard.

"We sewed it at night," explained the captain. "It slowed us down nicely."

"They were too proud to notice," said the captain of the King's ship. "Heroes are like that, and they always die uselessly. They bleed a lot, as well. Remember that, lad, keep your pride in check or it'll let you down."

And with that he pointed at the coast.

"That's Ywerdhon, the river Lifi. Welcome, a thousand thousand welcomes!"

24

Tara

They soon landed, and horses were brought from a nearby enclosure. Before long everyone was mounted and under way. Twenty miles of rich country passed, and then they came to Rath na Riogh, the hill Jago called Tara, the seat of the High King.

Jago saw a hill crowned by two circular earthworks. A wooden fence surrounded a complex of buildings from which rose smoke and the shrill cries of children at play. Pigs and geese wandered about at will, and on either side of the great wooden gates were heaps of stinking refuse. The gates looked strong enough, although they gave the appearance of not having been closed for ten years or more.

As soon as the travelers were spotted, a great cry went up and a horde of scraggy children and youths surged forward, chattering excitedly.

The King's captain used his whip to clear a path through the crowds and hustled the horses into the stockade.

Jago followed, keeping well in the background and making sure his harp was secure from the dozens of prying fingers. The children fired questions at him, but as their voices were shrill and their dialect strange, Jago did not reply—except to cuff a few of the more persistent ones over the ears.

He heard a drawling comment, followed by girlish laughter. Looking around, he saw a group of young women eyeing him.

121

They laughed impudently when he ignored them. Jago knew they spelled mischief. The only woman he felt at ease with was Mabby Trenoweth, and she was just a child really. As he thought of Mabby, he forgot his surroundings. Who would help her in her lonely vigil now that he was so far away? He felt guilty leaving her.

"What's the matter, gone deaf?" It was the captain standing there in front of him. "The King is in the hall, come in."

He took Jago past the smoky buildings, avoiding the puddles and animal droppings, until they came to the grandest building in the compound. Built of wood, it had a high sloping roof, with beautifully carved and painted eaves; the walls were smooth and similarly decorated. But that was nothing compared to the gorgeous splendor of the interior. There were rich tapestries and ornaments everywhere, and although the floor was littered with sleeping dogs, ash, gobs of mutton fat, and old bones, it was a kingly place.

There were long tables, seemingly covered in bundles of old clothes, and a sound that reminded Jago of the bees at swarming time.

Then he realized that the "bundles" were the slumped forms of sleeping people. Men and women, they were all fast asleep! Even the guard by the raised throne at the head of the hall was nodding off; his helmet clanged gently against his spear shaft.

"Errr? . . . hruup . . . oh yes, the King? Well he's just left, went up to his chamber. Can't be disturbed until mealtime."

"Come on," said the captain. "I smell new wine."

"And we can all see its work," said Jago.

They walked through the kitchens, where greasy scullions were lolling about and a few old women were bending over large, steamy caldrons. They soon found the wine. It was still in piled barrels, just as it had arrived from the port.

"I'll wager this load came this morning. Look, they've got

through three barrels already. Grab those horns and we'll have a swig."

It tasted good.

"Ah!" said Jago. "So this is Rath na Riogh, eh?"

"Yes, but you wait until the feast!" said the captain.

"It is *not* as I thought it would be," said Jago.

"Whatever is?"

After they had refreshed themeslves, they wandered around the town. Jago knew that, like the Giants' Dance and Carnac, Tara was special. Here he should come across the final event in his journey, the event that would make him strong enough to fight the sorcerer with some hope of winning.

As he walked, he realized that the place was larger than he had first thought. To the west he could see, a few miles distant, the silver thread of a river lying peacefully between green slopes. In the fields were herds of fat cattle and groups of sheep and goats; in the woods, pigs with their striped piglets. All was rich and peaceful.

Gradually a rhythmic chanting sound came from the pathway up the hill. A line of old men in brown and gray robes approached, walking slowly. They must be priests of some kind, Jago thought. He watched them eagerly. Perhaps this was something to do with his journey. But they passed by him with no sign of recognition.

"Holy men from the hills," said the captain. "Today is the day they petition the King to re-establish their rights for the coming year."

"So the King's awake by now?"

"Probably not; his steward usually deals with such minor matters."

"Minor? Is the struggle between good and evil a minor matter?"

The captain shrugged. "You have to define good and evil. What's good for some is evil for others."

"But how do you decide?"

"We respect the priests and what they have to tell us, but in the end we all have to make up our own minds. The King's word is law and sometimes it conflicts with what the priests say."

"But who do you listen to?" insisted Jago.

"Depends on who's paying for the feast, and today it's the King. So let's go in and enjoy ourselves!"

25

Minstrels' Feast

A gong sounded. Everyone began to make their way to the hall, which was already crowded when Jago and the captain arrived.

The place was in an uproar. It had come alive as if by magic. Gone were the snoring figures; instead there were nobles and warriors, all laughing, shouting, and singing. They thumped the tables to attract the attention of the regiment of serving boys, who ran with platters piled high with steaming food and great jugs of wine.

"This is your place, lad. See you later," said the captain, and went off.

Jago understood. Now that the court was formally in session the strict observance of custom had to be maintained. As a penniless traveler of low rank, Jago sat at the bottom of a side table with other humble wanderers. The King had placed above them his free herdsmen and pigmen, who actually sat at the end of the main table.

Jago was interested to see the captain placed quite near to the King, but to his surprise he noticed that the man next to him was none other than Cumail Conan, the pirate leader. And a few places down, he recognized Hiernan, the harpist, and other pirates. The captain laughed and chatted with them as if they were old friends. What was going on?

"Those men there," he muttered to his neighbor. "They're pirates!"

"Quite likely they are," replied the man. "But this is a special place and all are welcome here, landless, lordless, and lawless too. It's one of the great things about Ywerdhon—one day they're fighting to the death, the next they're feasting together. Many of the pirates have royal blood, you know."

Jago listened. He had forgotten about the food and was able to snatch only a few mouthfuls before it was carried away.

"Ach, the miserly Erse," said a Brabantine sailor.

"Wait, friend," said a fair-headed Saxon mercenary. "That was just to wake you up. The real feast starts after the contest."

"What contest?" asked Jago.

"Oh, why are you men of Kernow so ignorant about the ways of other nations? The song contest, you fool. And you with your old homemade harp! Give us a tune to whistle, Map Kernow!"

"Hush, the King speaks."

The King stood up. He was a noble figure with bronze hair and a small gold crown. He spoke slowly so that all the people could hear and understand. To make things easier for the guests, he interspersed his dialect with phrases in Kernewek, Kembri, Saxon, Flemish, and Greek. He announced that today there were only two principal contestants for the prize: a man from Ywerdhon and a man from Kembri. He hoped that others would sing after them, since the contest was open to all.

To Jago's annoyance, the first singer turned out to be the pirate Hiernan, the very man who had sneered at Jago's harp. He stood forth, dressed in a golden cloak. His red hair was bound with a fillet of gold set with gems; his harp was a splendidly ornate instrument, with a back that resembled a swan's neck. He began to sing and everyone listened intently. It was a familiar song that should have begun:

Mal ad-rualaid iathu marb
mac soer Setnai . . .

A prince has gone to the lands of the dead,
the noble son of Setne . . .

But instead of the usual names and ancestry, Hiernan skillfully interposed those of his own King, with fulsome com-
ments on his greatness and generosity. It became a song in
praise of the King, the kind of song that could be expected to
win such a contest. The applause was long and appreciative.

The man from Kembri stood up next. His language closely
resembled Jago's own. He glanced at the Queen, smiled, and
began:

> *Cyneifin ceinaf amser,*
> *Dyar adar, glas calledd*
> *Ereidr yn rhych, ychyng*
> *ngwedd, Gwyrdd mor*
> *brithotor tiredd.*

A great roar of pleasure went up from the throng. He was
calling Hiernan's bluff by adapting another famous lyric, this
time in praise of the Queen.

> *O May day, fairest of seasons;*
> *Loud are the birds, fresh are the grasses,*
> *Plows are in furrows and oxen yoked,*
> *the sea is green, the fields mottled.*

May, of course, was the Queen's name!

They listened as the man sang with all the artistry and cunning of his face. He created in the audience a longing for
things past, a wonder at things present, and a desire for things

to come. The judgment would be difficult. A song in praise of the King was clever; a song in praise of the woman he loved, even more clever.

After the applause, a steward rose to his feet and declared that the contest was open to one and all. It was no easy challenge. The preceding singers had been of exceptional wit and quality; no one would risk looking a fool against them.

Jago never knew what it was that made him call out. Certainly he did not consciously intend to do anything like that. The hall fell silent; all eyes were turned on him.

Jago stood up and unlaced his threadbare harp case. In silence he prepared the instrument and made the long walk toward the King's dais.

Hiernan recognized him and scoffed. He whispered to his friends, who sat back, grinning, to witness the disgrace of this peasant upstart. As Jago passed the captain he smiled, but it could not conceal his nervousness.

The steward nodded in an offhand manner, and a stool was brought forward for Jago to sit on. Jago bent over his harp and tried each string. He felt the instrument come alive in his hands. He had no idea what to sing, what would please the King.

Jago started to play, and as he sang, he felt it was the harp rather than himself that chose the words and notes.

The other two had sung of the King and Queen, but Jago sang of the land, of the earth from which they came and to which they would return. The song poured scorn on the works of men, on the futility of greatness and pride in the face of death. But it was not a sad song. It was a song of the joy of life, of the good earth, the wheat, the herds, water and wine, feasts and heroes.

The hall was entranced. It was a long time since a mere boy had come and sung so sweetly.

Jago sang of Tara and its greatness. He compared it to a

flower that must die at last, and ended with a verse in Kembri that everyone had heard, a prophetic verse:

> *Tair priforsedd beirdd ynys prydain*
> *gorsedd Meol Meriw*
> *gorsedd Beisgawen*
> *a gorsedd Bryn Gwyddan.*
>
> *Three foremost shrines of the island of Britain*
> *are the circle of Meol Meriw,*
> *the place of Boscawen,*
> *and the shrine of Bryn Gwyddan.*

The three names rang through the hall like a spell. All had heard them, all knew that when those places came to prominence, Tara the great, Tara the magnificent, would be doomed.

There was a stunned silence. Then tumultuous applause broke out. Men leaped to their feet shouting with emotion. They raised horn after horn of wine and drank to Jago's victory, for he had touched their hearts. The others had been clever. Jago had been true.

Jago was led forward and given a seat of honor. The King took a solid gold torc and placed it around his neck. It was very cold and very heavy.

The feast began in earnest. Whole roast pigs and sides of oxen were brought in, piles of steaming fowl, heaps of bread, gallons of wine, mead, and beer.

Jago noticed that the King ate very little and sipped at his wine rather than drinking it. He overheard the Queen say, "Eat, show a good example to our guests."

"I will try, but the lad puts me in mind of our daughter and her sorrows. How I wish that . . ."

The rest was lost in a roar of laughter, for a group of jugglers had run into the hall, turning somersaults and whooping.

Jago gazed down the long tables. He had never been in such a grand place before or sat down to eat with so many people. The travelers set up a cheer when they saw him, and the captain smiled. But Hiernan glowered, and the man from Kembri muttered to himself over a bowl of wine.

Jago felt a twinge of remorse; he had not meant to cause anyone any hurt. And he had not yet discovered why he had come here. His thorn stick, which never left his side, had not reacted to anything that had happened. It remained cold and still.

26

The Brindled Sow

The celebrations went on, until at last Jago excused himself to go to bed. The captain had pointed out a line of small huts by the side of the hall, where travelers could rest. It seemed that most of the people intended to stay up and continue their eating and drinking. They would probably fall asleep into the remnants of the feast, and sleep through to the next one.

Jago found a hut with a simple narrow bed. It was warm, so he removed his clothes and lay down. As he was dozing off, he heard a series of noises, rising and falling and rising again. Babies! Could he have chosen a place right next to a hut full of babies?

Suddenly he sat upright in bed. What was it? The strangest thing was happening. Through conflicting sounds he heard words. He listened carefully and began to repeat them to himself: "The . . . brindled . . . sow . . . of . . . Ull . . . nalee . . . in . . . moon . . . light . . . caught . . . your . . . wishes . . . brought . . . will . . . be!"

What an odd thing to hear. Jago decided he'd better get up and try and memorize it properly:

> "The brindled sow of Ullnalee
> in moonlight caught,
> your wishes brought
> will be."

131

Jago grabbed his stick and went to the entrance. He lifted the cowhide that served as a door, and gasped with surprise.

A full white moon was shining in the night sky. The sacred Hill of Tara was bathed in a luminous glow. Then, as he watched, some stray clouds scudded past, chased by a high wind. The moon's face disappeared behind them.

A snuffling grunt came from a nearby thicket, and a large sow came bundling toward him. Jago took his opportunity and leaped on the animal as she passed, but her coat was slippery and he fell with a thump onto the turf.

The sow moved off and Jago followed her down the hill. Near the bottom she stopped and stood quietly. Jago noticed that she had a large ring through her nose. It seemed to be the only part of the animal he could catch. But how? Of course, his stick.

He raised it cautiously and advanced on the sow. Then, suddenly, he thrust it forward, like spearing a fish. The stick slid into the ring and Jago was able to hold the struggling animal.

The clouds parted and the moonlight advanced in waves down the hillside. It reached where they stood, and covered the sow until she was silver. The stick began to vibrate as the moon power flowed into it. Jago jerked as if stung by a snake. The sow shook herself free and ambled off. Taking his thorn stick, he left without a word and made his way through the morning mists, down to the golden river. There a little coracle waited, impatient to ride once more on the swelling crests of the open sea.

27

Mazes

While Jago had been traveling in search of magical power, Mabby had been discovering all she could about the tower of Pengersick. She knew that one day they would have to enter there to strike at the sorcerer, and that a knowledge of his castle would be very useful.

But after the loss of his ring, the sorcerer had taken extra precautions to defend his black secrets. Mabby had tried to visit the place but a feeling of terror had caused her to flee. False doors and passages had been constructed to catch the unwary; and on some floors, trapdoors and other devices had been added. The tower was guarded by vigilant new demons.

For a long time, Mabby had wondered how she could get inside the castle again. Then one day as she was out walking, she heard the thunder of approaching hoofs. It was the Dark Lord, mounted on his black demon stallion, and alone.

Mabby hid herself in a hedge. The sorcerer whistled and looked about him. The only answer was a feeble croak. A wounded crow came flapping down and fell exhausted by the gleaming hoofs of the horse.

"Help me."

"What news have you of my ring?" demanded the sorcerer.

"None. But please help me. I was caught in a snare, I'm badly hurt."

"Fool! How dare you come to me with no news. Get out of my way!"

The wounded bird tried desperately to fly, but the sorcerer hit out at it with his whip and it fluttered back to earth. He wrenched the horse's head around and rode off.

As soon as he had gone, Mabby rushed forward. The bird was seriously hurt, she could see that. She picked it up and, cradling it in her arms, took it home, where she put it in a box in front of the fire. Then she tended its wounds and fed it milk. The bird opened its eyes and looked at her in surprise.

It said, "Thank you, kind girl. That evil man, how I wish we had not listened to him. He swore to give us all sorts of good things, and, to those of us who were enchanted he promised bodies once more."

"Bodies?"

"Yes, we are under an enchantment. We need bodies to live in, as your soul lives in your body. He promised to give them to us."

"But how? Whose bodies? You mean human bodies?"

"Oh, if only you knew the wicked ways of that man. He can take fresh-killed humans and put our souls into their corpses by spells. He can take people prisoner and, by pulling out their souls with hideous magic, leave a gap for ours to enter. He can change men into toads, snakes, and crows."

"How can one resist him?"

"He has a dark secret. I don't know what it is. But in his dungeon there is a gold box, and out of it comes a light, a strange light. We think it is the source of his evil power."

"How I wish I could see it."

"Ah, girl, that's impossible, unless you know how to get in there."

"Do you know?"

The crow coughed. Its body heaved in pain.

"It's my only secret . . ." it said, then fainted.

Mabby went and sat down. The bird knew. If only it could live, if only it could tell her. She said a prayer for the crow, and began thinking of how best to nurse it back to health.

"Mabby! Child-vean, come here!" It was her old mother calling.

"Oh, Mam, I can't, here's a sick bird needing care."

"Child, your father's well-being comes before any bird's. His leg is troubling him, and there's the tax money to take down to the crossroads."

"But, Mam, the poor bird . . ."

"Get along with you, Mabby. The money's got to be paid now or they'll turn us out of house and home. What could you do for sick birds then? No one cares now that we have always owed our allegiance only to the Earl. We'll die on the moor with no land to till."

Mabby remembered her duty. Jago had told her that she must look after the old ones. With a sadness in her heart, she went and took the copper coins from the table.

"Hurry back now, child! Don't linger in the lane."

Mabby needed no encouragement. Clasping the money in her hand, she ran as fast as she could down to the crossroads.

The soldiers had set up a trestle table there and all the country people were lining up to pay their taxes.

"Move along, move along. Now, Kit Polkinghorne of Trevean, six mazes."

"It was four last year."

"But this is this year, and it's six. Pay up!"

Grudgingly the man paid out his money. Cash was hard to come by in the country. To get it, one had to market and sell a hen or a bushel of wheat.

"Next, Tinner Basset of Polruan. Three mazes and a pig of tin. What's this, Tinner? This tin pure?"

"Upon my heart. Here, master, here's a mite to drink your health with."

The soldier frowned. He was sure the tin was of poor quality, but the copper coin that the tinner slipped him was enough to stop him looking too closely.

"Next, Silas Trenoweth of Trenoweth. Four mazes."

Mabby put the coins on the table.

"These are for my father, he cannot come."

"If he cannot come, then you owe us another coin for our trouble. Or we'll settle for a jug of beer. Well, girl?"

Mabby blushed. The soldiers enjoyed baiting the poor folk.

"We haven't got money or beer."

The soldiers roared with laughter, delighted at having worried her. Mabby turned, nearly in tears. The country folk looked on. They were angry, but powerless to do anything.

The soldiers jeered as Mabby ran off. They soon forgot her, though, and turned to torment another.

Mabby hurried back. She was worried about the sick bird. She arrived too late.

"Oh, Mam, oh . . ."

The bird was dead.

"Set up a terrible squawking and pecking, it did. Just before its black soul fled forever. Made a right mess of the box."

Mabby looked and saw that the crow had pecked some lines on the side of the box. She looked again, and could hardly conceal her delight. To anyone else it would have been a mess, but to Mabby it was the thing she wanted most of all at the moment. It was worth more to her than a pile of gold, or a new dress, or a warm shawl. For the bird had marked out for her with its beak a crude map of the secret passages of Pengersick Castle.

"Poor, kind, noble bird."

"The child's mad. Get rid of that thing before your father sees it. It'll anger him to see one of them here."

28

The Path Begins to Wind

On the north coast of Kernow a huge mass of black and yellow rock jutted out into the Celtic Sea. On either side of this headland, which was very nearly an island, were rocky-sided coves; and it was into one of these, Merlin's Cove, that Jago's coracle drifted after his crossing from Ywerdhon.

There was a gently shelving beach at the base of the towering cliff. To one side, Jago noticed a cave. He dragged his small skin boat across the sand and hid it inside.

It was cool and wet in the cave. In the rock face above it was a flight of narrow steps that led up to the walls of a castle, a fortification that seemed to grow out of the rock itself.

Jago stared up at it. The winds and tides to which he had entrusted his frail boat had landed him here, under Dyndajel, the unhappy home of the long-lost Earl of Kernow. Many years ago, the Earl had left to journey overseas with a picked band of adventurers. He had not returned.

Jago began to climb the steps. They were wet and slippery, with little between them and the sea washing the cove below. Once he looked down by mistake; the drop made him dizzy.

As he climbed, Jago became aware of a high, beautifully clear voice singing from the castle grounds. Eventually he reached a wooden door set in the sheer wall. There was no other way ahead. He tapped three times on the door with his fist.

The singing stopped. Jago heard voices, bubbles of laughter, and the rush of feet. Bolts shifted rustily and the door creaked open.

"Welcome . . ."

". . . to Dyndajel."

Jago frowned. Was this a trick? Was it one voice or two? Was he seeing double?

"Don't worry . . ."

". . . we're twins."

Jago smiled, relieved.

"My name is Jago Blythcroghan. I've just landed in the cove down there. Is there a way out?"

"Wet . . ."

". . . or dry?" they said.

"Dry, for preference. Tell me, why do you speak like that?"

"Like . . ."

". . . what?"

"Oh, never mind."

He followed them through the door, waited while they bolted it carefully, and went up some more steps into a small walled garden that lay in the shadow of the keep. Here, on a bench, sat the most beautiful lady Jago had ever seen. She was dressed in green and had long red hair. In her hand she held a spindle, and around her was a pile of sheep's wool. She stopped her work when she saw Jago, and looked in amazement at his stained clothes, his dusty wolfskin cloak, and his harp in its sailcloth case.

Jago shuffled uncomfortably. After all, he was no longer a child. He should have taken better care of himself. His hair needed combing and his face needed a good wash. He moved from foot to foot, trying to hide the fact that his leather moccasins were dreadfully worn. The lady was so clean, beautiful, and fresh.

"And where have you come from?" she said kindly. "Twins, go and fetch something to eat and drink. Please sit down."

"His name's Jago . . ."

". . . Blythcroghan!" they said, and ran off.

"I see you have a harp, and that wolfskin. Surely it cannot be the prophecy! You are so young!"

Jago did not reply. The lady seemed to know something about him. He put aside his thorn stick and harp case and undid the fastening of the cloak to let air around his neck. He was hot from the climb. The sun glinted off the gold torc; its richness contrasted strangely with his threadbare tunic.

When she saw the torc, the lady jumped up with a look of surprise on her face; her green eyes gleamed as bright as sunlit quartz.

"It's all coming true." She seemed excited.

The twins arrived with a crescent-shaped pasty and a clay jug of sweet goat's milk.

"Sit down and eat, Jago Blythcroghan, and listen to what I have to say. Many years ago, the Earl, my husband, left this sad land for Sarcenia. He went to help the Emperor fight against the mountain men and shamans on the Eastern Border. He never returned. We know he is still alive, but he is under a wicked enchantment. Last quarter, we received a message saying that if we could pay ten thousand gold mazes, then he would be freed. But the gold maze is a rare coin since the Earl left us so many years ago. There cannot be ten thousand of them left in the world, let alone Kernow. Especially since that evil man in Penwith, the Lord of Pengersick, has been on the rampage."

"Pengersick!" Jago said. His eyes went cold.

"Yes, you have heard of him? Well, listen, I had a dream just after the message telling me that a champion harper would find us the ransom. You see, before he left for overseas, the

Earl buried a large amount of treasure somewhere in the castle grounds. Alas, he did not tell us where! Can you help us find the gold? Do you have any skill in the magic arts?"

"Magic? Well . . . Look, I can give you my neck ring, that's solid gold."

"That is kind of you, but it is not the answer to our problem. To give your torc would mean denying the generosity of those who gave it to you. And valuable as it is, it would not be enough. No, it is the hidden treasure that must be used to save the Earl."

"To tell you the truth," said Jago, "I have been on a journey. I have amassed a certain amount of magical power. I'm not a sorcerer. It's for a reason, it is to destroy a great evil. I do not know if it is enough for the battle before me, and to use any of it would be to risk disaster. I must save all I have for the final contest."

"I see . . ." A great pain came into the lady's eyes. The twins hung their heads and began to weep. They did not understand what was happening, but they could tell that their mother was deeply distressed.

The lady shook her head and smiled. She had fought and overcome her anguish, and now appeared placid once more.

"Tell me about your journey. You came by boat?"

"A small skin boat that I found in Ywerdhon."

"Where did you go to in Ywerdhon? Sianion?"

"No, although I have heard tell it is a mighty place. I went to Rath na Riogh, the Hill of Tara."

Her flickering eyes betrayed her interest.

"The King himself gave me this torc."

"He is well? And my . . . I mean the Queen, she's well?"

"Yes," said Jago. So that was it! She was the daughter they spoke of so sadly.

"Look," he went on, "I've been thinking about this hidden treasure of yours. Perhaps my magic will be enough to find it and defeat the Lord, too. There may be a reason I came here that I do not understand. Kernow has sorely missed the Earl."

"Oh, thank you, thank you."

"Have you any idea where to look?" asked Jago.

"I'll call the old man." She rang a bell. After a few minutes, a very ancient-looking man came walking slowly into the garden. He had long white hair, a white beard, and tiny mouse-like eyes, which stared at Jago.

"Good," he said, after inspecting Jago for some time. "Such a poor and landless fellow is bound to rid Kernow of its sickness. You see, he has no property to lose. Property is the curse of this land!"

"Where do we look for the gold?" asked the lady.

The old man held up a small, thickish, bronze coin.

"The maze! This is the only clue."

Jago took the coin, and as he did so, a thrill of recognition ran up his arm. The coin felt warm and soft; Jago could feel the steady pulsing of a small heart. He grabbed his thorn stick from the ground, and the two lives, that of the wand and that of the coin, met inside him. They flowed together and mingled and created a picture in his mind.

"Hush," said the old man, as the twins began to clamor for information. But Jago heard nothing. He started to move, his wand outstretched as if it were a nail being attracted toward a magnet. He went out of the garden and into the castle courtyard, where people stopped in surprise, before a compulsion to join the procession took hold of them. Jago led the ever-growing crowd past the keep, past the stables, and out of a sally port onto the bare cliff top. He noticed no one and nothing. He walked alone through the invisible turns and twists of what seemed to be a large labyrinth. Finally he stopped by a well, and turned toward a low wall that sheltered an acre of vegetables from the sea winds.

"Here," he said quietly. "Dig here."

The old man snapped his fingers and three gardeners hurried forward with spades.

"Start digging, lads!"

And they set to, wielding their long-handled shovels eagerly. At last there was a "clunk."

"Wood! A plank!"

They scraped the plank clean and lifted one end of it.

"A pot!"

The pot came out of the ground. It was quite light and was sealed with red wax.

"Look, on the wax, that's the mark of the Earl's ring!"

"Open it, quick," said the old man.

They cut away the wax and opened the pot. There was a groan of disappointment.

"Where's the gold?"

Inside were a handful of tiny, black, shriveled things and a piece of soft leather, wrapped around something solid. One of the men undid the package and found a sphere of rock crystal: a clear, glassy stone in the shape of a globe.

"Go on digging," ordered the old man.

Jago and the lady looked at the contents of the pot, as the gardeners resumed their delving.

"These look like some kind of seeds. And that crystal looks like a scrying stone."

"What's that?" asked Jago.

"You don't know? It's for fortunetelling. Some people can see pictures in it."

Jago looked at the crystal distrustfully.

"I prefer magic that lets you do things, not just know about them."

"Knowing about things is useful, too," said the lady.

"Another pot!" exclaimed a gardener.

"And another!" shouted his friend.

"That's what I mean," said Jago. "I like the kind of magic that gives substantial results."

As the pots were taken out of the hole, they crumbled and broke. A great shower of gleaming gold flooded onto the black earth.

The watchers were stunned into silence; the sight brought tears of joy to their eyes. They fetched a pile of leather bags and counted the gold into them. The stack of full bags grew.

Jago smiled, but he was feeling tired and a little weak. A black frame seemed to force itself around his eyes, so that all at once he appeared to be looking down a long tunnel at the scene before him. A rushing sound filled his ears and the excited chatter of the people was muffled, as if it came from a long way off.

The old man stepped forward and gently took Jago by the hand. Jago started to shiver, as if cold; but he was hot, so hot that sweat lined his brow and neck.

"Sit here, put your head down low, right down." The old man held Jago's neck firmly.

"What is it?" whispered the lady in fear.

The old man said, "He's a brave boy. He's got great power but he has to learn how to use it. This is the first time, the most dangerous time. Let him rest now. He'll wake up fit, but part of his power will be gone forever."

Jago heard what the man said. As they carried him off to a quiet room, he thought about it. It had been his choice. He could have refused. But he was glad he had helped them.

When he woke up, he saw that the old man had put the dried seeds, the crystal, and the gold on a nearby table.

The old man was standing by the bed.

"Well, and how do you feel?" he asked.

"Well enough, thank you," replied Jago.

"Jago Blythcroghan, may I ask you the reason for your

journeys? It's not everybody who would do such a difficult thing alone, and for no profit. What is your aim? You can tell me in safety."

"There's no harm in my telling you. You are a wizard, are you not?"

"Well now, that's a big word for a little knowledge. All I can do is a few tricks. I've a lot to learn yet."

"Perhaps, but you are far ahead of me."

"That's it, then. You have started on the Way, too?"

"Yes, sir. I have started on the Way. But I started alone."

"It always happens alone. A teacher can sometimes be useful but he cannot have experiences on your behalf, and you are nothing without experiences. All the books on magic are so much scrap parchment without the experiences. Take some warnings. Know, Will, Dare, Be Silent. The Path is very difficult at first; then it splits into two forks. You have to decide which to take."

"Tell me something. If you are a wizard, why didn't you discover the treasure yourself?"

"It was buried for you alone to discover. It was your first test."

Jago sat up in bed angrily. "Test? Is that all? Have I wasted my power for nothing? Look here, I'm not a traveler in these dangerous ways to play stupid tricks. I have a purpose. I mean to smash the power of Pengersick, once and for all."

The old man's eyes veiled over at the mention of Pengersick. "Ah, Jago, Jago, I can see you're no longer a boy but a man. A man is someone with a purpose in life. No, your power wasn't wasted. It's all part of the web of dreams."

"What on earth is the web of dreams?" asked Jago, more confused than ever.

"Each man has his own. Now, we've got work to do. Are you feeling strong enough for a journey to Sarcenia? It's a free ride. I promise it won't diminish any more of your power."

"Another journey?"

"A different kind of journey. We've got to deliver the gold and make sure we ransom the Earl."

"How?"

The old man chuckled. He stamped his foot three times, and one of the great stones that made the floor rose out of it and hovered a foot or so above the ground.

"Now for a good old Kernow trick, young lad!

> *"Go stone*
> *Fly wind*
> *Come cloud*
> *Eyes blind*
> *Clear mind*
> *Go stone."*

Jago was lifted onto the stone. The bags of gold clinked down beside him. Tightly gripping the old man's surprisingly strong legs, he was terrified to see the walls turn to cloud. They were flying on the stone. Looking down, Jago could see fields and woods, with flocks and herds. They passed a port, crowded with masts, and skimmed far above the sea. The sun was hot and Jago soon stopped shivering. Beautiful and strange were the lands and cities they passed, and there were thick forests and mountain ridges, too. Jago had not thought the world was so large.

"Slow this thing down, old man, or we'll fall over the edge of the world."

"Don't believe it. The world has no end!"

"No end? Surely it must have. It has a beginning."

"Save your breath, lad-vean, here's Sarcenia. It's such a long time since I was here. There's the desert and some lions, too. Bless me, look, the palace."

Jago gazed in wonder at the marble building, shining from

amid a forest of towers and turrets. It was like a dream, with golden domes, emerald gardens, and silver pools.

But it appeared totally deserted. Down went the stone, landing on a mosaic pathway among aromatic shrubs.

"It would have taken an ordinary man a year of hard travel to reach this sublime spot from Kernow. And cost a great deal of money."

Jago stared at the building in front of him. The bright sunlight that shimmered all around seemed frozen as it struck the white, pale green, pinkish beige, and gold of the building.

Terraces and arbors of crystal led the eyes onward: past courts where jade-green cypresses threw cooling shade over pools and tinkling fountains; up avenues of delicate stone tracery, whose screens broke up the sun into mosaic patterns.

The building itself was symmetrical, and so finely balanced that it seemed to be made of ice; slim towers rose into the blistering heat, by the side of flame-shaped domes of beaten copper were lace-fine fans of masonry, growing from the structure like white stone trees.

The old man nodded with pleasure. "Pure reason, pure abstract thought. No crude carvings of man or beast; just the inevitable, balanced line. Ahh, it does my eyes good to look on it once more!"

"Where are we?"

"The Palace of Memeliz, home of Emir Dawood el Kebir Yussuf."

"Is the Earl imprisoned here?"

"Let us see."

29

Falling Feather

They walked up to the palace and were met by an enormous black-skinned guard, clad in red-enameled armor. The guard made strange grunting noises. Jago realized he could not speak, for his tongue was missing.

"Salaam aleikum! El Kebir?"

The guard bowed briefly and led the way. They went through the richest and most breathtakingly beautiful halls Jago had ever seen. Compared to them, the castle rooms of Dyndajel were peasants' huts.

They entered a light, scented hall where a black-bearded man was dozing on a velvet sofa. The guard coughed, and poured hot black liquid into small ceramic bowls before leaving.

The man sat up and smiled. He was dressed in silks and red leather slippers.

"We've brought the gold, Dawood el Kebir," said the old man.

"What gold?"

Jago was surprised to hear the Emir speaking Kernewek.

"The treasure, the ransom for the Earl."

The Emir threw back his head and laughed, showing his fine white teeth.

"Gold? What do I want with gold?"

"The treasure, the hidden treasure."

147

"Oh, you Franks, gold will be your death. I meant the real treasure. The gold was only a marker . . ."

"The contents of the first pot?"

The Emir looked interested. "Yes, what was there?"

"Just an old crystal."

"Anything else?"

"Some bits and pieces . . ."

"You've wasted your journey coming without them."

"What about the Earl?"

"Gwynion Kerdroya? He's not here. Ask Jowan Tremelyn, he knows all about that. It was a long time ago. But please, drink!"

The old man looked suspiciously at the smiling Emir.

"Wait a minute! You're telling me you don't want the gold, but only the contents of the first pot? And that the Earl isn't here anyway? And you say that Jowan Tremelyn has him? But the Earl *was* here, so Tremelyn must have been here, as well."

"That's true," replied the Emir.

"A wasted journey," said Jago angrily.

"I think not," said the old man. "But our problems are complicated by this news. Tremelyn left Kernow with the Earl many years ago. But I know someone whose black arts savor of this place. He must have learned them here. I do not know what your involvement is, El Kebir. But I don't trust you."

The Emir smiled. He shrugged and sipped his drink, then he spoke. "I must declare my interest. The man Tremelyn stole my daughter's heart. He eloped with her. They were married by a renegade priest. She was of age and was willing; indeed I wager it was her idea. What could I do? I put a curse on both of them."

"What are you talking about?" demanded Jago. "Who are all these people? Who is this Jowan Tremelyn?"

The old man gave Jago a meaningful look. But Jago's face was suddenly powerful and stern; it frightened the old man.

He saw in it a grim determination that could only end in disaster.

"Of course!" said Jago. "I see it all now. But can it be true? The man who holds his own Earl captive, the man who has learned evil magic from this emir's daughter, this Jowan Tremelyn . . . he is the sorcerer! The Dark Lord of Pengersick!"

Jago looked at the Emir, who smiled and popped a date into his mouth. He pushed the bowl toward Jago.

"Have one. They're really delicious."

The old man turned to the Emir and said sternly, "Well, since you do not have the Earl, you can't have the treasure. Be it gold, crystal, or dried-up seeds!"

A glint came into the Emir's eyes. "Oh dear. I'm sorry if I misled you. But I did tell you where he was, after all."

"I suppose so," said the old man reluctantly.

The Emir raised his drink to his lips.

"Stay awhile. Refresh yourselves."

"Thank you," replied the old man, "but we must go."

"Before you leave, there's something I would like to try. A little augury."

"A little what?" asked Jago.

"Fortunetelling," explained the old man. "Go ahead, El Kebir. But quickly."

The Emir got up and walked to the door. He led them out into a small courtyard.

"Look!" shouted Jago. "A trap!"

Standing in the center of the courtyard was a familiar and sinister figure, swathed in a long black cloak. He stood silent and unmoving. Pengersick!

Jago realized with a jolt of fear that he had left his thorn stick back in the room at Dyndajel. Was all his trouble for nothing? Was he to be trapped here like this, weaponless?

"Don't be alarmed, Jago," said the old man. "Watch."

He walked up to the figure and tapped him on the head. It made a hollow noise.

"It's just an empty shell, an effigy."

"I don't care what fancy words you call it—just as long as it isn't the Dark Lord."

"It's merely a clever deception."

The Emir coughed and started speaking. "I once read a book from Kernow, brought here by the Earl actually, called *Princess Esmeralda*. Do you know it? Well, in it was a trick that I'm going to try now. I'm going to drop a feather from up in that tower. Let us see upon whom it falls: the effigy of the Lord of Pengersick or this young lad here, who is so eager to get back and do battle with him."

"How childish," muttered the old man.

"I'd like to see it," said Jago.

The Emir gathered up his silken robes and ran quickly to the top of the pointed tower. He held out his hand and let drop a small feather, which wafted through the air.

Jago stood stock-still, not far from the cloaked effigy of the Sorcerer of Pengersick.

The feather drifted this way and that: now it was over Jago, now over the effigy. Upon whom would it fall? On him, or his greatest enemy?

Down, down, down, came the feather, until it hovered just a little above Jago's head. He held his breath with excitement.

But it was not to be. A gust of wind came from nowhere and diverted the feather onto the black shoulder of the sorcerer.

Jago gulped in disappointment. Then the old man shouted, "He's gone, he's tricked us. Quick! Back to the stone."

Jago looked up to the tower. The Emir had disappeared. While they had been watching the feather, he had secretly stolen away.

"He's bound for Dyndajel, I'm sure of that. Whatever it was

he wanted, he's certain to get it now. We can't hope to reach the castle before he does. But let's hurry."

Off they went like lightning, but they were still too late. As the stone hovered back into the room and the walls closed around them again, they noticed that the shriveled seeds were missing from the table.

"It was those things he was after," said the old man. "I thought so. I wonder what they were?"

Jago leaped off the stone and picked up his thorn stick, his wand. He was glad to see it safe.

"What we found out does not change my mind," said Jago. "In fact, it makes my plan to defeat the sorcerer all the more urgent, for it seems that he has the Earl captive."

"What can we do to help you?" said the old man.

"Nothing. This is meant to be my battle."

They found the lady and told her what had happened. A council was formed, and pompous men stood up and made long speeches. Jago slipped out of a door and found the old man waiting outside.

"It's no good," said Jago. "You can send deputations to all the outlying farmsteads and granges to discuss the problem; you can talk about the amount of crossbows and men-at-arms you are due—but I have a score to settle with Pengersick. I've helped you all I can, and now you must look to your own affairs."

"Right, boy. Let them talk, it makes them feel useful. When they've finished, our soldiers will ride south. If they don't help in the fight, at least they can clear up afterward."

Jago grinned. He gathered up his thorn stick and cloak.

"Take care of my harp, would you? If I don't return, give it to someone who can use it."

And so he left the castle.

30

Blades in the Night

Jago sat at the entrance of the cave, looking out at the storm clouds that raced across the dim sky. He felt sad as he watched the wind wrench the dying leaves off the branches. They looked for all the world like small brown soldiers falling in battle.

Perhaps at the end of the coming battle he himself would be dead, for had not the feather landed on the effigy of the Dark Lord, not on him? It seemed to Jago that the fates had chosen the sorcerer as the victor. Still, there was only one way to find out.

The leaves were dying. It had been summer when he had first challenged the Dark Lord on the cliff of Cudden; now, all over Penwith, the sorcerer's forces were securely entrenched to last out the winter. Jago had thought of ways of putting off the struggle; but, no, it had to be soon. There was no way he could remain hidden throughout the winter.

He heard Mabby coming through the thorn bushes. In the two days since he had returned to Mabby and the cave, he had memorized the map that she had drawn from the crow's pecked-out sketch.

"What of the small folk from Bal Dhu and the other mines?" he asked, as they settled down by the fire to eat.

"Terrible things happened while you were away. There were two serious rebellions in the mines, but the elf slaves

152

found they couldn't throw off the Dark Lord's forces. His stoats and ferrets hunted them most cruelly. Many of the little folk broke out, but a great force of them was ambushed as they fled to the Lesart. They were turned into stones. They litter the moors down by Polkimbro. The sorcerer turned the young ones into pebbles, and then had them scattered on the shore. I've collected these from Loe Bar."

She went to the dark corner of the cave and brought out a wooden box filled with the most beautiful pebbles Jago had seen. It was obvious from their shape and luster that they had elf life locked within them.

"The foul beast!"

"I know, Jago. We've all suffered in some way. There are many, though, who would still dare to fight him had they a leader to show them how."

"Let's see what we can do for these little ones."

Jago stook up his thorn stick and concentrated his thoughts on freeing the elf children from their stony prisons. His mind hit a black mass, a sticky mass, and struggled with it like a man fighting thick mud. At last he broke through. The pebbles began to move as tiny hearts started to beat inside them. Slowly, but visibly, their shapes changed to those of small elf children.

"How are we to look after them?" asked Mabby, thrilled at the magic she had seen.

"We can't. But we can find their parents. Now I know what to do, I can bring all the elves back to life."

And so he did. He crept out into the countryside, and when he reached the rough moor near Polkimbro, he raised his wand and began to sing a soft tune he had learned from the wind. As he walked, he let the end of his stick trail over the stones that littered the ground. His magic worked and the elf breath locked within the rocks began to stir; hearts beat once more, and the stones began to turn back to elves.

By nightfall he had led an army of elves back to the cave. Other bands of the little folk came from far and wide when they heard what was happening.

The elf leader stepped forward. Jago smiled as he recognized Mungo Pygal.

"Stars and shadows, friend Mungo," said Jago.

"Stars and shadows," whispered Mungo, with tears in his eyes.

"Is the battle to be soon?" asked Mungo.

"Indeed it is. Tonight! I'm glad you have all come well armed. Listen, friends, much has happened since you marched away down the tunnel that day. This is Mabby Trenoweth. She has braved Pengersick in his castle to discover his secrets while I journeyed forth. Know that I have put my feet on the Way. I have some power, but I sorely need your help. You must get me inside the castle. Mabby has a map."

Mungo and his officers studied the parchment excitedly.

"What defenses, friend Mabby?"

"The woods are watched by crows, ravens, rooks, and choughs. Among the briers and bracken are posted stoats and ferrets. The gatehouse is guarded by soldiers with dogs. There are more soldiers inside, and more dogs. But the dungeons are lightly defended."

Mungo whistled. "And what else?"

Jago smiled. "We all know the Dark Lord has great and evil magic, but he has a weak spot. He has to draw his power from somewhere, and we think the secret is hidden in the dungeon. After dealing with him and his men, we must hasten down there and prize that secret from its dark corner."

Mungo grinned with anticipation. He and his fighters had waited a long time to get to grips with the sorcerer. He turned to his men and issued orders in the Elven tongue.

The night outside was wild and windy. Large billowing clouds raced across the full moon.

Mungo insisted that his men be sent in to deal with the first outposts, and Jago agreed. The attacking force crept toward the pine trees that surrounded Pengersick, the elf soldiers slipping in groups from shadow to shadow, so that they were never seen. Jago, his wolfskin wrapped around him, looked and felt like a wolf. He felt all the warlike cunning of the pack leader whom he had slain enter his own actions and instincts.

Jago had ordered Mabby to stay at home, although he knew that she would disobey. Anyway, she would be invisible and reasonably safe.

A few of Mungo's best scouts wormed their way forward into the undergrowth to deal with the stoat guards and other sentries. Minutes later they reappeared with blood on their short swords. Jago was able to witness the next part for himself. Elf archers moved up, and soon the air was full of twanging strings and whirring arrows.

There was a peculiar thumping sound as a shower of dead birds hit the soft turf, each with an elf bolt through its heart or brain. Soon the forest floor was covered with their black bodies. So swift and accurate was the shooting that not a bird managed to call out a warning. As the army ran softly through the pine trees toward the castle ditch, Jago smelt an acrid odor. He saw elves bending down by some ferret holes with small pots that smoked and spluttered.

"What's that?"

"Poison. Quiet!"

The ditch was soon lined with elf soldiers. Jago saw the moon glint off their armor and spear points. From the gatehouse came the snuffling of dogs and the clink of chains.

Jago looked back in alarm. He had noticed several furry shapes creeping up behind them. He nudged Mungo, who smiled at his concern. One of the furry creatures came close, and Jago saw that it was an elf wearing the skin of a newly slain stoat. The group passed over the ditch and edged right up to the gatehouse. One of them made a howling noise, which set the dogs yapping.

The gate creaked open. The disguised elves fell back into shadow, as two guards with dogs emerged.

"Hey, Ripper! Hey, Gutslit! Quiet, you curs. It's only the wind in the grass. Stupid hounds!"

There was a low whine, cut short by whistling noises and strange splashes. From his vantage point in the ditch, Jago saw the two dogs fall stone dead. The guards bent to examine them, and so did not notice the shadows move. Again the whistling noise, and the men crumpled up with poisoned arrows sticking out of them. One of them choked, trying to sound the alarm. He crawled toward the gate; but at a silent signal from Mungo the elf host was upon him. However, it was Jago who got there first, and who dispatched the wretched fellow with a slash of his flint knife.

The gate was now unguarded.

"Get into your positions. Haffer, take your archers to the kennels. Moxa, go to the barracks with fire and poison. Darnel, come with me to attack the tower. But send half your men to help Raith open the stables and panic the horses. No one to fire or run until the signal!"

Jago waited, his cheek pressed against the rough wood of the gate. Around him the little soldiers scurried to their positions. He wiped his knife on the side of his tunic and gripped his wand tightly.

31

Death to Arluth Dhu!

Mungo looked up at the moon. He raised a silver elf horn to his lips and blew a shrill battle cry.

The elf hordes ran yelling and shouting into the attack. Jago heard a medley of sounds break out: the crackle of fire; the curses of stricken men; the screams of the dogs; the terrified neighing of the horses, as they broke out of the stables and trampled on the guards who had come stumbling out at the alarm.

The moon threw a shaft of light onto the ghastly scene. The elves were taking their revenge.

"Come with me, Jago. Into the hall!"

The assault group, with Mungo at their head, burst into the great hall of the castle, where a surprised group of guards were milling about in front of the roaring fire.

Now the battle took a grim turn. The men could see their attackers and pulled weapons off the walls to deal with them. They grabbed blazing logs from the fire and sent them bouncing and hissing among the elf ranks.

"A Mungo among them!" yelled the elf leader. It was his ancestral cry. He drew a wicked-looking scimitar from its snakeskin sheath.

Jago was everywhere at once: leaping and striking and slashing and snarling like a wolf.

A volley of elf bolts sang across the hall. Men dropped screaming to their knees as the poison burned their blood. Mungo's sword whistled and fell without pause. He was oblivious of everything: the fire, the arrows, the swords, the spears.

"The dogs, watch for the dogs!"

The sorcerer had suddenly appeared and unleashed half a dozen of his strongest and fiercest hunting dogs along the gallery.

They came bounding down the stairs, their red eyes rolling and their long fangs dripping with excitement. The guards in the hall took this opportunity to escape up the stairs; the elf troops paused for a moment in fear.

But the dogs did not pause. With a horrifying burst of howling they were among the little folk.

Jago shouted with rage as he saw the dogs break into the elf ranks and scatter the warriors into the air like rats. The stone floor was slippery with blood.

"Aim, aim straight," called Mungo sternly. And he gave the lead by grabbing a bow from a quailing archer and sending a shaft humming toward a cur. The animal let out a shriek as the poison began to bite.

Their confidence regained, the elf archers sent in volley after volley of lethal arrows. Soon the dogs were in retreat. Grimly the attackers chased them, determined to show no mercy.

Jago had other things on his mind. He found himself halfway up the stairs to the gallery. Behind him clustered a group of elf soldiers and at the top of the stairs, silent and towering with wrath, stood a figure in black. The Dark Lord of Pengersick.

"Stay and fight," yelled Jago, as he moved toward the sorcerer.

The sorcerer scornfully pointed his beringed finger at Jago.

A flash of white fire leaped down the stairs and hit him full in the chest.

Mungo called out in despair as Jago was covered in flames. His cry was echoed in anguished tones by the other warriors.

The fire subsided. Jago remained where he was, a faint smile on his lips.

A look of doubt washed over the dark face of the sorcerer. Up to now, he had regarded the attack on his castle as mere sport and had enjoyed the cruel battle.

Jago ran up the stairs. With a yell of delight, the elf soldiers scampered after him, pausing only to fire arrows into the billowing cloak of their arch-enemy.

"He runs. The sorcerer runs!"

The cry echoed around the great hall. It struck terror into the guards and made the elves fight with redoubled ferocity.

Now began a hunt along dark passages and stairways. The elf soldiers began to sing a victory song as they fought, sensing that the enemy was in mortal dread of them. They hunted men and dogs down like trapped rats, until corridor, hall, cellar, and gallery echoed to shouts and screams.

Jago, Mungo, and a dedicated band ignored the other enemies and kept on after the Dark Lord. They followed him up to the highest tower, where a desperate rear guard was fighting off the victorious elf troops. The sorcerer trampled his own people underfoot to get to the open battlements.

But there was no relief. A host of falcons and hawks waited there to take their revenge. They swooped on the guards and dogs with razor-sharp talons and cutting beaks, till their enemies threw themselves off the tower in agony.

Cutting their way through the struggling mass by the door, the small party burst out onto the battlements. They stopped. There, on the edge, stood the Lord of Pengersick. As they watched, he summoned up his evil power to bursting pitch.

Then he screamed a word. A dreadful word, which made the earth tremble in fear and the winds moan in terror. A word whose evil profanity burst on the struggling throng, knocking senseless both man and beast, friend and foe.

Jago was pushed back by the power of the word, his outstretched arms protecting his elf comrades. His wolfskin cloak was almost torn off him by the evil force.

Time itself stood still. It could have been five minutes or five seconds. All that Jago saw was the figure of the Dark Lord, floating in space.

Time started again with a bump. The body of the sorcerer cartwheeled over the battlements and crashed through darkness to the courtyard, a hundred feet below.

Jago turned and raced down the way he had come. Mungo was not far behind him. As they ran, they heard screams and bone-crunching thuds from the courtyard. The elf troops were busy dispatching the last of their enemies from the tower.

Jago and Mungo could find no sign of the sorcerer among the piles of broken bodies on the ground.

"Quick, down to the dungeons!" said Jago.

They found the well and bucket, and descended. Eventually they came to the room where the strange light streamed from the filigree gold box.

"He's not been here," said a voice.

"Heaven's butterflies!" said Mungo. "Is that a ghost?"

"No, just me," said the voice, and Mabby appeared. "I've been down here all the time, waiting in case anyone tried to steal the source. Come and see."

Mabby took them across to the box. Mungo whistled in amazement. Jago's eyes gleamed. Neither of them had seen anything like it. It must surely be very important. Inside they could see a squat, dark shape.

"What evil natterjack is that?" asked Mungo.

"It's a toad," said Mabby.

"How do we open it?" asked Jago.

"I think I know," said Mabby proudly.

Out of her sleeve Mabby took the ring, the Black Sigil of Pengersick. Its black star gleamed in the cold light.

Carved on the side of the box, among the other patterns, was a similar five-pointed star. Mabby put the ring against it. It fitted perfectly.

"So the ring is the key!" exclaimed Jago. "Well done, Mabby."

"Turn it. Let's see the natterjack," said Mungo, his hand ready on his small sword.

Mabby turned the key. The box lid sprang open and the cell was flooded with a brilliant, burning light.

Mabby slipped the ring onto her finger and gently lifted out the toad. It was an ugly creature, with a slimy knobby skin.

"Poor thing, how long has that evil man kept you locked up?"

The toad jumped out of Mabby's hand and landed on the floor. Mungo drew his sword.

"No!" said Jago. "Wait. Look what's happening."

The toad seemed to grow and change shape, until it was no longer recognizable in its original form. In its place stood a man—a tall, regal man, with a lined face and a straw-yellow beard. He had brown eyes, which contrasted strangely with his light hair. He was dressed in a rich robe. On his finger was a gold ring and around his neck a twisted gold torc.

"Thank you, dear girl," he said.

Jago realized that the elf leader was kneeling.

Mungo said gravely, "Welcome home, Earl of Kernow. Welcome home."

32

Ending

The Earl looked gravely about him, at the little room and at the assembled elf soldiers. His bright eyes noticed their weapons, and their wounds.

"You will forgive my ignorance," he said. "I have been locked in mysterious dreams for so long. Where am I? The last I knew I was sheltering from a storm in a cave of the tideless sea. The battle had been fought and won, but there was treachery in the air."

"The battle has been fought and won again!" declared Mungo.

"And there is still treachery in the air," said Jago.

"You are in a secret place under the castle of Pengersick," explained Mabby.

"Pengersick? Then Tremelyn was right!"

"The battle was fought against him. He had subjected this land of Penwith to cruel tyranny. He has used evil magic to gain control of the people."

"Then you were right to fight him," answered the Earl.

"There can be no doubt of that," said Mungo grimly.

They made their way up to the castle gate and looked at the destruction. The blaring of horns was heard and lights were seen entering the valley.

"That will be the men from Dyndajel. Too late, but they can

help with clearing up and guard duties. All your brave warriors deserve a good rest, Mungo," said Jago.

"So do you, friend Jago."

Jago whistled and Hanno came swooping down. The boy and the bird were joyfully reunited. Jago whispered to him and the falcon took off with a cry of delight.

"We shall soon have him. My brave bird will alert his friends, the night-mousers. They will seek him out and tell us."

"Enough time tomorrow, lad," said Mungo.

"No. It has started and has not been finished. It must be finished soon. He cannot get away from us now!"

"We will need horses. The men from Dyndajel will lend us theirs."

The horsemen from Dyndajel were kneeling in rows; alongside them stood men-at-arms, with their long spears, and the archers and slingers in leather jerkins. The old man who had taken Jago to Sarcenia was there, too. He had ridden through the night in a litter slung between two mules. It had been his action that had urged the men to move at last.

From the pines came the hoot of a hunting owl. A white, ghostly shape came flitting through the trees. The old man raised his arm and the owl landed on his wrist. The two of them, the old man and the owl, held a silent conversation, and then the old man said to the Earl, "The sorcerer has been traced."

The Earl called Mungo Pygal to his side.

33

The Unknown Battle of Jago Blythcroghan

Jago stood by his horse. He was restless. In the courtyard they had lit pine flares, which made it as bright as day. Some of the new arrivals were helping by patrolling the battle ground; others were engaged in dragging out the bodies of the dogs to burn beneath the trees. Half a dozen roaring pyres were already sending their thick smoke up into the clear night sky.

Jago gazed up at the stars he knew so well and let forth a deep sigh. Why hadn't he attacked the sorcerer when he had first caught sight of him at the head of the stairs? He had missed his chance. Now the fiend had escaped.

The Earl came over. He had had a hurried conference with his officers and with Mungo and his lieutenants.

"He was seen making for the shaft complex by the cliff. Mungo knows a way into the labyrinth. It's through an old tomb, a barrow. We can take only a few people—you, myself, Mungo, and two of his best trackers. We leave immediately."

Jago was quite content to let the Earl and Mungo have conferences. After all, they were commanders and had the right to act like that. As for himself, he wished for only one thing: the defeat of the evil one, and peace forever after. Things were still far from decided. The feather of fate had not yet landed. It hovered there in the air. Upon whose shoulders would it fall?

Jago's wand hummed with power. It had expended very little energy in the battle, since Jago had used his flint knife. The wand seemed patient, awaiting the outcome.

They were off now, the horses clattering across the cobbles: past the groups of exhausted elf folk, bathing their wounds and sleeping; past the sentries from Dyndajel; past the funeral pyres with their ghastly shapes spluttering in the dark; and past the huge crowd of curious countryfolk who had assembled in their thousands, some armed and ready to help.

As they recognized the Earl, a great cheer rose from the throng. They realized that at last they were free from the sorcerer.

The Earl talked to them as he went by. He bade them seek out the elf kind and help them with food, drink, and medicines. And then he rode on.

After a while, they came to a cliff near the sea. They dismounted while the trackers sought out the way to the ancient barrow. They soon found it, and pried open a stone from its side. Jago had spent many a happy summer afternoon lazing on these same cliffs, but he could not remember ever having seen the barrow.

Into the cold black hole they went, not daring to speak for fear of disturbing the ancient spirits that slept there. Kernow was full of such places, and they were best left alone. The elves led the way down a corridor. It was like a mine adit. They relaxed, feeling totally at home now they were underground again.

"Starlight and shades, this is a cold place," remarked the Earl.

Jago was silent. They turned into a gallery that sloped down and down.

Jago stopped and listened. He had heard a rushing sound. Then he noticed a foaming wave sweeping up to meet them.

"Look out for the water!" he yelled.

"What water?" asked Mungo. "Why, the floor's as dry as a bone."

"The water!" exclaimed Jago, as he saw it break over his feet in a silver flood. It soaked his ankles and rose up his legs.

"There's no water, Jago," said the Earl kindly.

A look of understanding had entered Mungo's eyes. "Hush," he said. "For him there is!"

Jago struggled against the water, which now lapped around his neck and tore at his clothes, with hard, liquid fingers. It was as cold as gold. And as real.

With a mighty effort, Jago pulled himself free, and followed the elf scouts along the tunnel.

Again Jago hesitated.

"What is it now, friend Jago?" asked Mungo.

"Fire!"

"Fire?"

"Yes. Great sheets of flame, making the rocks melt and drip. The air is as hot as a dragon's breath. It's scorching my hair, my skin! Aaagh!"

Jago bent almost double. He held his wolfskin over his head and pushed against the intense heat. The cloak was scarred and blackened by the fire.

The Earl and the elves saw it happen. They looked on in horror as Jago reeled and staggered. The Earl grabbed Jago's arm and tried to help him. And although the Earl himself was not burned, he actually felt Jago's cloak smolder and char.

They ran with him through the fire and stood panting in a passageway that led to the sea. The sound of the breakers could be heard, transmitted to them by the rock walls of the tunnel.

"The treasure room," said Jago.

Now he remembered it. It seemed a long time ago: when he had dragged his wounded leg down these very same underground passages.

They glanced into the tiny room. It was empty. Marks on the floor showed that some heavy object, a wooden box perhaps, had been dragged in, and then out. If Mabby had been with them, she would have recognized the incense that still clung to the room.

"He's been here, sure enough. Taken something out, his treasure maybe . . ."

"Where's he gone?"

"It's high tide. He could have a boat under the cliff."

The sorcerer must have found the tunnels going to the sea. A perfect escape route.

They were not far down the passage when the snakes struck.

Jago faced them grimly. Knowing that the others did not see the dangers he faced, he did not waste breath on explanations. He was fighting a different battle in a different place. It was a world overlaid on the one that everyone else knew. Only he and the sorcerer lived in that other world.

The snakes were large, sinuous, and terrifying. Jago brought his wand into play and blasted them with its magic power, until the stench of their burning bodies filled the narrow place.

"What's that smell?" complained one of the elf scouts.

"Quiet, fellow," was all that Mungo could say, for he knew that Jago was fighting a private battle, and even though they wanted to help, they were powerless.

At last all the snakes were destroyed. Jago ran past the scorched remnants eagerly, with the others close behind him. They saw the little square opening in the cliffs, leading to the sea. Jago's eyes gleamed, for standing alongside the gap was the dark bulk of the sorcerer.

Jago's companions stopped. With almost imperceptible motion their mouths fell open and their slow fingers came up to point. Jago had left them behind in the normal world of space and time. He stood alone and faced the sorcerer. The

Dark Lord smiled and with a sweep of his arm silently invited Jago to share in his power, in his diabolical world. For a twinge of time Jago was tempted. In that second, he felt an affinity, almost a blood relationship with the sorcerer; for had they not both traveled and suffered upon the same Way?

A feather lay upon the Dark Lord's shoulder. Jago saw it, gasped with pain, and with an effort rejected his enemy. He glimpsed the divide in the way—the left hand and the right hand. He threw forward his wand.

There was a sulfurous flash, as if lightning had struck, and for a split second they saw the black shape of the sorcerer, hovering between earth and an eternal chasm of evil.

Then all was quiet. The others feared for Jago—but then realized that the flash was of his doing. It was not directed against him, but by him. By him against his enemy: the Dark Lord of Pengersick.

"What happened?" asked Mungo.

Jago sat down. He looked tired, drained of life.

"I don't know, but I do know I hit him with all the power I had."

"There's blood here," said one of the elf scouts excitedly.

"And a burned shred of cloak."

"He must have fallen into the sea."

"It's too dark to see anything."

"Nothing on earth could have survived that blast!"

Mungo reached up and put his arm around Jago's shoulder.

"Come, lad, let's find a place to rest."

And rest they did, while the whole of Penwith, in fact the whole of Kernow, took a holiday to celebrate the victory. The splash of blood and shred of cloak proved the sorcerer's death, so they all said.

Jago was not sure, but he kept his thoughts to himself. The Earl offered him much gold and land. But he refused it. All he wanted was to return to his former life, to become a simple pony boy again upon the moors.

The Earl returned to Dyndajel. Peace and contentment reigned in Penwith, and the fair land of Kernow breathed free again.

The tower of Pengersick was locked and barricaded. It was unnecessary to forbid people to go there: they still shunned the dark place. The lands over which the sorcerer had ruled were returned to the Earl, and he redistributed them among those who had remained loyal to him.

The Trenoweths were not slow to accept the Earl's bounty. They bought a small, comfortable house in Hellys, and settled down to a life free from want. Their little croft grew dirty and neglected, and the stony fields they had spent their life tilling became overgrown with weeds. In time, the Trenoweths began to despise Jago's lack of worldly ambition, his soiled clothes and simple tastes.

But not Mabby. She was hurt and mystified by the reaction of her parents. And, worse, Jago didn't seem to care.

Mabby, who still retained her magic power, decided to use it actively for good. She distributed portions of her parents' newfound wealth to the poor, but she did it secretly, invisibly. And she waited for the gloomy mood to vanish from Jago's mind.

Several weeks after the first anniversary of the destruction of the sorcerer's power, a pony emerged from the neglected woodlands surrounding the tower. A tousle-headed boy dismounted to stand and stare at the empty windows, the sagging rafters.

As he gazed at the scene, his troubled expression relaxed. Time had not stood still here as he had feared it would; its ravages were evident. That was what he had come to see, the sorcerer's tower subject to the same laws as everything else. He smiled at the broken eaves, the paving stones fringed with grass, the stains of tempest and sea fury on the corroded walls.

His fear that the sorcerer's power was not really dead, his fear that the tower itself would be stronger than time itself— that fear now evaporated, dissolved to nothingness, left no trace.

Jago Blythcroghan felt free at last. For a year he had wandered with the fear of the place hanging on his back like a sticky burr. The burr was gone—he was free.

He laughed to himself, kicked at a tussock of rank grass, leaped up onto the pony's back, and rode away as fast and as joyfully as the pony could go.

Glossary of People, Places, and Things

ARLUTH DHU   Dark Lord
BAL DHU   Black Mine
BOSVENEGH   Bodmin
BOTHY   small hut or cottage
BRETAN VYGHAN   Brittany
CARREK LOS YN COS   the brown rock in the wood: i.e., St. Michael's Mount
DERMOT   free man
DUBHGALL   dark stranger
DUNHEVED   Launceston
DYNDAJEL   Tintagel
EDGEWORDS   ogham, an ancient form of writing
EMLYN   ermin
ERSE   Irish
FRYNK   France
GIANTS' DANCE   Stonehenge
GOONHILLY   moor pony
GWYNMAEN   white rock
HELLYS   Helston
HERNYETIS   a lost town of Lyonesse
JOWAN   John
KEMBRI   Wales
KERDROYA   maze or labyrinth
KERNEWEK   Cornish language
KERNOW   Cornwall
KIDDLEYWINK   public alehouse
LESART   The Lizard
LIFI   River Liffey
LODENEK   Padstow
LYONESSE   a lost land off the coast of Cornwall

MAP KERNOW   son of Cornwall
MARGHAS YOW   Marazion
MAZE   an ancient coin with a shepherds' dance or Troy design
MENHIR   a tall stone
MOUNTAMOPUS   a lost town of Lyonesse
NANSCES   the land of the newly dead
PELLAR   spell-binder
PEN AN WLAS   Land's End
PENGERSICK   pengassick, the head of the marsh
PENSANS   Penzance
POLKIMBRO   Welshman's pool
PORTH IA   St. Ives
PORTHQWYN   a lost harbor near Southampton
RATH NA RIOGH   the Hill of Tara
SARUM   an ancient settlement near Salisbury
SAWSEN   English
SHAMAN   a priest or priest doctor
SYLLAN   the Scilly Isles
TREMELYN   homestead of the mill
TRENOWETH   new homestead
YWERDHON   Ireland
ZAWN   a valley, a rocky cleft running to the sea